FROM THE NANCY DREW FILES

THE CASE: *Nancy's boyfriend, Ned, takes a job as an insurance claims investigator and ends up the target of an investigation—for the murder of Toby Foyle.*

CONTACT: Ned *might not be cut out for detective work—but he's definitely not cut out for murder, either.*

SUSPECTS: Michelle Ferraro—*Toby's fiery girlfriend saw him with another woman—and now she's seeing red.*

Dr. Robert Meyers—*the physician who filled out Toby's accident report stands to lose his practice if the claim proves false.*

Wally Biggs—*Ned's boss. He's accused Ned of being irresponsible, but is he just covering up his own crime?*

COMPLICATIONS: *Nancy has to find a way to prove Ned's innocence, even though the police found him at the murder scene—and his fingerprints were on the crowbar that killed Toby Foyle.*

Books in The Nancy Drew Files ® Series

#1 SECRETS CAN KILL
#2 DEADLY INTENT
#3 MURDER ON ICE
#4 SMILE AND SAY MURDER
#5 HIT AND RUN HOLIDAY
#6 WHITE WATER TERROR
#7 DEADLY DOUBLES
#8 TWO POINTS TO MURDER
#9 FALSE MOVES
#10 BURIED SECRETS
#11 HEART OF DANGER
#12 FATAL RANSOM
#13 WINGS OF FEAR
#14 THIS SIDE OF EVIL
#15 TRIAL BY FIRE
#16 NEVER SAY DIE
#17 STAY TUNED FOR DANGER
#18 CIRCLE OF EVIL
#19 SISTERS IN CRIME
#20 VERY DEADLY YOURS
#21 RECIPE FOR MURDER
#22 FATAL ATTRACTION
#23 SINISTER PARADISE
#24 TILL DEATH DO US PART
#25 RICH AND DANGEROUS
#26 PLAYING WITH FIRE
#27 MOST LIKELY TO DIE
#28 THE BLACK WIDOW
#29 PURE POISON
#30 DEATH BY DESIGN
#31 TROUBLE IN TAHITI
#32 HIGH MARKS FOR MALICE
#33 DANGER IN DISGUISE
#34 VANISHING ACT
#35 BAD MEDICINE
#36 OVER THE EDGE
#37 LAST DANCE
#38 THE FINAL SCENE
#39 THE SUSPECT NEXT DOOR
#40 SHADOW OF A DOUBT
#41 SOMETHING TO HIDE
#42 THE WRONG CHEMISTRY
#43 FALSE IMPRESSIONS
#44 SCENT OF DANGER
#45 OUT OF BOUNDS
#46 WIN, PLACE OR DIE
#47 FLIRTING WITH DANGER
#48 A DATE WITH DECEPTION
#49 PORTRAIT IN CRIME
#50 DEEP SECRETS
#51 A MODEL CRIME
#52 DANGER FOR HIRE
#53 TRAIL OF LIES
#54 COLD AS ICE
#55 DON'T LOOK TWICE
#56 MAKE NO MISTAKE
#57 INTO THIN AIR
#58 HOT PURSUIT
#59 HIGH RISK

Available from ARCHWAY Paperbacks

THE NANCY DREW FILES™

Case 59

HIGH RISK

CAROLYN KEENE

AN ARCHWAY PAPERBACK
Published by POCKET BOOKS
New York London Toronto Sydney Tokyo Singapore

This book is a work of fiction. Names, characters, places and incidents are either the product of the author's imagination or are used fictitiously. Any resemblance to actual events or locales or persons, living or dead, is entirely coincidental.

AN ARCHWAY PAPERBACK *Original*

An Archway Paperback published by
POCKET BOOKS, a division of Simon & Schuster
1230 Avenue of the Americas, New York, NY 10020

Produced by Mega-Books of New York, Inc.

ISBN: 0-671-70036-7

First Archway Paperback printing May 1991

10 9 8 7 6 5 4 3 2 1

Cover art by Tom Galasinski

Printed in the U.S.A.

IL 7+

HIGH RISK

Chapter One

NANCY DREW, I could kill you!" Bess Marvin's usually soft voice sounded annoyed as she took the armful of clothes her friend handed her.

"I never thought the day would come when *I'd* get tired of shopping for clothes," Bess went on. "But we've been at this for four hours already. We must have covered every store in River Heights, and you still haven't bought anything. You're driving me nuts!"

"Sorry," Nancy said. She came out of the boutique's fitting room, smoothing her reddish blond hair behind her ears. "I guess I'm not really in the mood to shop today."

"Obviously," Bess said huffily. She carried the pile of clothes Nancy had discarded and went out to hang them back on the racks.

George Fayne, Bess's cousin and Nancy's friend, was standing by the fitting room door, obviously bored. "Better get with it, Nan," she advised. "That is, if you want to find something new to wear for Ned tonight. It's four o'clock already." George bent forward, stretching her long, athletic body and shaking her head so that her short, dark curls bounced around her face. "Besides," she added, popping back up, "all this standing around is exhausting! Maybe I should stop bugging Bess about not getting enough exercise. I don't know how she can shop the way she does—I feel as if I've just run a marathon!"

"Okay, okay." Nancy grinned at her friend. "I promise to find something I like in the next ten minutes."

Both girls turned as Bess hurried back into the fitting area, carrying a mock-turtleneck dress made of peach-colored jersey.

"Look what I found. This is *it,*" she said with a decisive toss of her blond hair. "If you don't like this, then I give up."

Nancy took the dress and looked at it with a critical eye. "I don't know," she said. "The skirt is awfully short."

"Oh, you know you've got perfect legs, so what are you worried about?" Bess scolded, waving away Nancy's objection.

"Maybe I'm just modest." Nancy went back into the cubicle to try the dress on.

As she smoothed the soft fabric over her hips, Nancy gazed at herself in the mirror. Bess had made a great choice, she realized. The soft color brought out the pink in her cheeks, and her blue eyes looked even brighter by contrast. The skirt wasn't *that* short, she decided, and it made her legs appear even longer.

"Okay, guys, you're off duty," she called through the door. "Bess, it *is* the perfect dress."

"Hallelujah!" George exclaimed. "Hurry up and change, Nan. After this workout, even I need some ice cream."

A few minutes later the three girls were seated around a little wrought-iron table in front of an ice-cream parlor in downtown River Heights, the girls' hometown. George had ordered a sundae, Nancy a scoop of fudge swirl. Bess had ordered a diet soda, but now she was casting longing glances at George's sundae. Shorter and curvier than her two friends, Bess was perpetually trying to lose a few pounds, even though she was the only one who thought she needed to.

"So what's the big occasion?" George wanted to know. She ate a spoonful of her sundae. "What's so special about tonight that you have to go out and spend four hours looking for the perfect new outfit?"

Nancy shrugged. "It's no big deal, really," she said. "It's just that I want something that will really get Ned's attention. I've been feeling a little bit—well, neglected lately." She frowned. "Ned's job is kind of taking over his life."

Ned Nickerson, Nancy's longtime boyfriend, had a steady summer job at Mutual Life, a large insurance company in nearby Mapleton. This summer Ned had been assigned to the claims department. It was an important job, and he was taking his new duties very seriously. A little too seriously, Nancy was beginning to think.

"Yeah, he has been pretty tied up, hasn't he?" Bess commented. "I've only seen him once since he got back from Emerson."

"Tell me about it!" Nancy exclaimed. "He's been home from college for almost a month, and *I've* seen him only a few times! He works late almost every night. And when I do see him, all he ever talks about is life as a claims detective."

"Claims detective, huh?" echoed George. Her big brown eyes creased at the corners as she smiled. "So now we've got a detective duo—Drew and Nickerson."

At eighteen, Nancy already had an excellent reputation as an amateur detective. She had a natural talent for solving mysteries, and she loved doing it, too.

"Hey, you don't think Ned's stepping on your toes, do you?" George asked suddenly.

Before Nancy could answer, Bess cut in. "Oh, George, don't be silly," she scoffed. "Ned often helps Nancy out on her cases. I'm sure she feels the same way about helping him. Hey, Nan!" She turned to Nancy, her pretty face shining with excitement. "Maybe you and Ned should go into business together. Nickerson-Drew Investigations. Wouldn't that be romantic?"

"Nickerson-Drew Investigations?" Nancy arched a slender brow at Bess. "Why not *Drew*-Nickerson?"

"Whatever." Bess waved a hand impatiently.

Her smile fading, Nancy poked at the mound of ice cream in her plastic dish. "I don't know," she said slowly. "I'm not sure I like Ned's style. I mean, I'm glad he enjoys his job, but does he have to be so gung-ho about it? And he's getting really suspicious of people. I guess he comes across a lot of false claims, but it's weird to see him so distrustful when he's usually so sweet."

"Nan, are you going to eat that last bite of ice cream?" Bess broke in.

George laughed. "Bess's killer instincts never fail when it comes to ice cream."

"It's yours, Bess," Nancy said. She pushed the dish across the table, then glanced at her watch and stood up. "I should go. I'm picking Ned up in Mapleton in two and a half hours, and I have to get ready. See you guys later, okay?"

"Hey, Nan—knock his socks off," Bess called after Nancy as she walked away.

Nancy smiled to herself. With the dress she'd just bought, she hoped to do just that.

At seven-fifteen that evening Nancy pulled her blue Mustang up to the curb in front of the Mutual Life offices in Mapleton. Ned said he'd be waiting out front for her, but she didn't see him anywhere. Oh, well, she thought, he's probably on his way down. She made a quick check of her reflection in the rearview mirror, fluffing out her shoulder-length hair one last time. Then she sat back to wait.

Five minutes later there was still no sign of Ned. Fighting a twinge of annoyance, Nancy gazed out the window, letting her eyes run over the Mutual Life building complex.

Mutual Life had started out as a life and health insurance company. Then, about five years earlier, they had bought out a small car insurance company. After that, the original marble-fronted building just wasn't big enough to hold the growing business, so the company had built an ultramodern annex, which was joined to the original building by a glass-and-steel enclosed walkway. Nancy thought the annex was ugly, but she supposed it served a purpose.

By seven-thirty Nancy had checked her watch about twenty times and was getting irritated. She was about to get out of the car and go to his office when Ned came through the revolving glass doors of the annex and dashed over to Nancy's Mustang.

"Hey, gorgeous! Sorry I'm late," he said, bending down to kiss her through the open window. "I got caught on the phone."

At the sight of his handsome face and warm brown eyes, Nancy felt her annoyance melt away. "No problem," she murmured, looping a hand around his neck to catch another kiss.

After their lips parted, Ned went around to the passenger side and climbed in. Nancy started the car and drove off toward Conchita's, the restaurant they had planned to try that night.

"Wow, what a day," Ned remarked, loosening his tie and settling his tall frame into the car seat. "I spent most of it arguing with this woman who's trying to make Mutual Life pay for the face-lift she just got. Can you believe it? I tried to explain to her that health insurance is meant to take care of people's bills when they're sick, not when they want a new look. But she wouldn't stop bugging me. I'm telling you, it's amazing what people try to get away with."

"Mmmm," Nancy said in a neutral voice. It was great to see Ned so enthusiastic about his work, but she was a little disappointed that he hadn't even noticed her new dress.

"I had a talk with Joe Packard today—you know, the head of my department," Ned went on.

"About what?" asked Nancy.

"He says I'm doing a good job, but I shouldn't push myself so hard."

Nancy nodded. She wasn't the only one who thought Ned was too involved in his work. "Well, maybe you should listen to Mr. Packard," she said.

Ned shrugged. "I don't know—I don't think Joe's heart is really in the job anymore. He used to be a real dragon. Everyone said he made our department what it is. But now— His wife died a few months back. They were separated, but he must have still loved her. Andy, my office mate, says Packard hasn't been the same since then."

"Poor guy," Nancy said sympathetically. "It must be hard for him."

They parked down the block from Conchita's. "So what did you do today?" Ned asked as they walked up the street.

"I went shopping with Bess and George,"

Nancy told him, smoothing the skirt of her peach dress with one hand. *Now* he'll notice, she thought.

But Ned just nodded. "That's nice," he said, and immediately went back to talking about work.

Nancy held back a sigh. I get just as single-minded when I'm working on a case, she reminded herself. Ned always listens to me. So I can listen to his problems at work for a change!

"I'm so glad we're finally eating here," Nancy said as they entered the restaurant. She was looking forward to trying Conchita's. It had opened a few months earlier, and she'd heard it had great Mexican food and a terrific atmosphere.

Glancing around, she knew she wouldn't be disappointed. The place was nearly full. Colorful sombreros hung on the walls, and stuffed cloth cacti rose nearly to the ceiling. An old-fashioned jukebox was blasting music by mariachi bands, while waiters and waitresses in embroidered vests bustled through the festive room. They and the guests all seemed to be enjoying themselves immensely.

"Hey, this looks great," Ned said as the hostess led them to a table. He sniffed the air. "Smells great, too. I'm starved!"

As Nancy and Ned were seated, Nancy noticed the girl at the table next to theirs because she was getting up to leave. The girl, a few years older than Nancy, maybe twenty-two, had carefully tousled blond hair that looked as if it had half a can of mousse in it. Her mascara was so heavy that her eyelashes looked like the legs of a spider, and her blusher made red bars on her cheeks. The girl's companion was a slender man of about twenty-five, with slicked-back hair and a mustache.

"I'll be right back, Toby," the girl said, giggling. "I'm just going to powder my nose."

"Don't be long, sweetheart," the man replied in a sugary voice. He blew the girl a kiss, and she giggled again.

"I'll get the car," Toby added. "But the night is still young. Shall we go dancing?"

"*Oooh,* yes, Toby," the girl cooed, then walked away with tiny mincing steps. Toby stood and headed for the door.

"Whew!" Nancy said, letting out her breath. "Talk about sickly sweet!"

Ned had noticed the couple, too, and he was frowning. "I know I've seen that girl somewhere," he muttered. "I just can't think of—Hey!" He leaned over and picked up a plastic card that was lying on the just-vacated table. "That guy left his credit card behind."

Nancy jumped up. "Maybe we can catch him—" she began, but she broke off suddenly and stared at her boyfriend.

The expression on Ned's face was one of anger as he stared down at the card in his hand. "That crook!" he said. Then he set off for the door.

"Ned, what's going on?" asked Nancy, confused. She hurried after him, but Ned didn't stop or turn around. He marched up to Toby and clapped a hand on his shoulder.

"Is your name Foyle?" Ned demanded.

"Yes, why?" Toby looked puzzled.

"You're supposed to be laid up, Mr. Foyle," Ned snapped. "You had a car accident a month ago, or did you forget?"

"An accident?" Foyle's eyes widened, and Nancy read fear in them.

"You got a hundred thousand dollars in damages, for head injuries your doctor said were so bad you'd be disabled for months. Maybe you forgot that, too," Ned went on angrily. "But I investigated your insurance claim, and *I* haven't forgotten."

"What are you talking about?" Toby Foyle took a step backward. "What accident? What money? You've got the wrong guy, mister!"

Nancy just stared at Ned. Why was he confronting this man, a total stranger, in the middle of their date?

"The wrong guy?" Ned repeated. "I don't think so. You put in a false claim." Nancy saw Ned's hands clench into fists at his sides as he growled, "You're in deep trouble, Mr. Foyle."

Chapter Two

TOBY FOYLE'S FACE turned the color of skim milk. "What are you, some kind of lunatic?" he shouted at Ned, putting his hands up protectively. "Get away from me!"

"I'm no lunatic," Ned said, glaring at Foyle. "But you're a fraud, mister."

"Ned, please!" Nancy could hardly believe what was happening. Could this furious guy be the Ned Nickerson she knew and loved?

By this time the entire crowd was silent and staring at Ned and Foyle. Suddenly a man in a dark suit burst through the front door. "I'm the manager. What's the trouble here?" he asked crisply.

"The trouble is, this guy is a maniac!" Foyle

cried. He pointed a finger at Ned, and Nancy could see that his hand was shaking. "He tried to attack me!"

"Ned didn't attack anyone," Nancy broke in, but the manager paid no attention to her. He turned to Ned with an accusing stare.

"Mr. Foyle here has gotten his hands on a lot of money illegally," Ned insisted. "I happen to know because I'm an insurance claims investigator. He stated he was disabled in a car accident, but he doesn't look disabled to me. I just want to see justice done."

Foyle was still pale. "I'm telling you, you've got the wrong guy!" he said again.

"Ned, there's got to be more than one Foyle in Mapleton," Nancy put in urgently.

"Look, I don't care what the gentleman's name is," the manager said, glowering at Ned and Nancy. "All I know is, he's a guest in my restaurant and you're harassing him." The manager jabbed a finger at Ned's chest. "I want you out of here *now.*"

"But—" Ned began.

The manager cut him off. "Now!" he repeated sternly. "Or do I have to call the police?"

Ned's jaw tensed. "You won't get away with this," he told Foyle. Then he tossed Foyle's credit card on the floor, turned, and stalked out of the restaurant.

Nancy was shocked and embarrassed by Ned's rude behavior. "I-I'm really sorry," she murmured to the manager. Then she hurried after her boyfriend. When she caught up with Ned, he was leaning against her car, scowling.

"What in the world did you think you were doing in there?" Nancy burst out.

"That guy is getting away with fraud!" Ned fumed.

Nancy drew a deep breath. How could he be so sure? "Move aside and let me unlock the car," she said. "Let's go to your house. We can talk about it on our way."

Ned went around to the passenger side and climbed in. As Nancy pulled out into the street, she asked, "Don't you think you could have made a mistake about who the guy was? Have you ever met him before?"

"No, not in person," Ned admitted. "We do most of our investigations by phone. But it wasn't a mistake," he insisted. "The name on the credit card was the same. T. N. Foyle. I remember seeing it when the claim came over my desk and thinking, T. N. Foyle—I wonder if people call him Tinfoil? How could there be two people in Mapleton with that same name?"

"I don't know, Ned," Nancy said, frustrated. "But how do you know that guy in the restaurant is even *from* Mapleton? There are lots of other towns around here. The point is, even if it *could* be the same guy, you didn't have enough evidence to go gunning for him the way you did."

"But I know I was right!" Ned said hotly.

Nancy blew out a breath with a whoosh. "Right or wrong, you still have to build a case—"

"Nan, I know you're a great detective, but please don't lecture me on how to do *my* job," Ned interrupted. He raked a hand through his hair. "If you think I was wrong, fine. Let's just not talk about it anymore."

Nancy clamped her mouth shut, feeling stung. Why wouldn't Ned just admit that he'd overreacted? She drove in silence until they reached Ned's street. Then she steered to the curb in front of the Nickerson house and stopped the car.

"Do you want to come in?" Ned asked in a chilly voice.

Nancy was hurt by his tone. "No," she retorted. "I think this date is pretty much over, don't you?"

"I guess so." Ned got out of the car and strode across the lawn to his front door.

Nancy watched him go inside. She was still sitting there a minute later when the porch light clicked off.

It was practically pitch-black on the street, thanks to the drooping boughs of the huge willows that lined the sidewalk and blocked the light from the street lamps. Nancy sat in the car for a few more minutes, staring into the darkness and trying to figure out what had gone wrong.

She'd been so happy to see Ned, but he'd hardly paid any attention to her. If only he wasn't on the job all the time, none of this would have happened. Why did he jump all over me when it's obvious he was wrong?

It *was* obvious, wasn't it?

Finally Nancy gave up trying to make sense of the whole incident and drove home.

Nancy slept poorly that night. When she awoke Friday morning to the sound of a ringing phone, she felt as if she'd barely rested at all. Groggy, she fumbled for the receiver.

"'Lo?" she murmured.

"Nan!" Bess's voice bubbled over the wire. "Rise and shine—it's after ten o'clock! How was your big date last night?"

"Mmmphh." Nancy groaned as her mind cleared and she remembered what had happened the previous evening. "It was a total disaster."

"What do you mean?" Bess sounded concerned. "Is everything okay?"

Nancy sat up in bed. "I don't really know. But if you and George come over for brunch I'll tell you all about it. I need advice."

"We'll be there in a little while," Bess promised, and hung up.

Nancy looked out her bedroom window, and her spirits rose a bit when she saw that the day was sunny and clear. After showering, she pulled on a T-shirt and a pair of blue shorts, then went downstairs.

The house was deserted. Nancy's father was at his law office, and there was a note from Hannah Gruen, the Drews' housekeeper, on the kitchen table: "Gone plant shopping. Back soon."

Nancy set to work frying bacon and collecting ingredients for French toast. Soon Bess and

George arrived, and the girls gathered in the kitchen. As Nancy made French toast, she told her friends what had happened the previous night.

"So I don't know what to do," Nancy finished. "Ned was totally out of line. But for some reason he got mad at *me.* He didn't even say good night. I think he expected me to side with him. But how could I? He was wrong!"

George gave Nancy a sidelong glance as she carried a stack of plates to the table. "Are you sure about that?" she asked.

"What do you mean, am I sure?" Nancy retorted. "He had no proof!" She piled the last slices of French toast on a platter and set it down in front of her friends.

"That coincidence with the names sounds pretty reasonable to me," Bess ventured, reaching for a strip of bacon.

"Oh, come on, Bess," Nancy said. "You've done enough detective work to know that a coincidence isn't solid proof."

"No, it's not, but you've worked with a lot less sometimes when you were solving a case," Bess pointed out.

"Bess is right," George put in. She poured syrup over her French toast. "Nan, I hate to say this, but are you sure you're not just a little bit bothered by the fact that Ned's job is a lot like what you do? You're acting as if you are."

Nancy's blue eyes widened. "You think I'm jealous?" she asked, startled.

George lowered her eyes. "A little," she replied

after a moment. "I mean, I think we're all agreed that Ned went too far last night. But he could be right about that Foyle guy. I think it wasn't the best idea for you to tell him he was wrong."

As she listened, Nancy realized that her friends were right. "You're saying I was trying to tell him how to do his job," she murmured.

"Maybe he sees it that way," Bess put in hesitantly.

"Right. Give him a little slack," added George, jabbing a piece of French toast and popping it into her mouth.

Nancy nodded. "I do understand what you're saying," she said slowly. "The fight we had wasn't all Ned's fault. Even though he acted badly, I shouldn't have come down so hard on him. After all, he's stood by me a billion times when I was following a wild hunch."

She got up from the table and added, "I'm going to call him right now." She dialed Ned's office number on the extension in the den so she'd have privacy.

"Ned?" she said when he picked up. "It's Nancy. I wanted—well, I just wanted to say I'm sorry about the way I acted last night."

"Oh, Nan." Ned's voice was tender, and Nancy's heart beat a little faster. "I'm the one who should apologize. You were right—I shouldn't have jumped in and accused that guy without evidence. I was just so mad I wasn't thinking straight. But I am now."

Nancy's spirits soared as Ned spoke. Now he sounded like the old Ned, the one she loved!

"Hey, I never did get dinner at Conchita's," she said into the receiver. "But I'll settle for any kind of dinner tonight—if I can have it with you, Nickerson."

"Sounds good. Listen, I have an idea," Ned began. Then he broke off to speak to someone in his office. "Yeah, I'll be right there.

"I've got to go," he said, speaking to Nancy again. "How about meeting me here after work? I have a plan for tonight."

"You're on! I'll be there at—six?" she asked. Ned said that would be okay. Nancy felt happy and relieved as she headed back to the kitchen.

"I think they made up," Bess commented to George as Nancy floated into the kitchen. "Look at the grin on her face!"

"Yep," Nancy said. "I think everything is going to be just fine."

At five minutes to six Nancy parked in the now-empty employee lot in the back of the Mutual Life annex. She hurried around to the door, went in, and presented herself at the reception desk, where a night guard was on duty.

The elderly man, who knew her by sight, waved Nancy past his desk. "I know Ned'll be glad to see you, young lady," he said with an indulgent smile. "Just go on up and surprise him."

"Thanks," Nancy replied, flashing him a grin. She zipped up the stairs to Ned's department, which was on the second floor of the annex. But as she breezed into the open conference area in the middle of the department, the cheerful greeting she had been about to utter died on her lips.

Nancy saw Ned's immediate superior, Wally Biggs, standing in the doorway of the office Ned shared with his coworker, Andy Feinberg. Biggs, a plump, oily man in his thirties, was shouting at Ned. Nancy winced as she heard his voice.

"It's the most idiotic, unprofessional thing I've ever heard of, Nickerson!" Biggs yelled. "Do you realize that your behavior in that restaurant last night will have a negative effect on the reputation of this entire company?"

"But I—" Ned tried to interrupt. Nancy craned her neck until she could see her boyfriend over Wally Biggs's shoulder. Ned's face was red, but Biggs wouldn't give him a chance to explain.

"Don't give me any of your excuses," Biggs ranted on. "I don't want to hear them. I was against giving you such a responsible position in the first place, and now I see that I was right. Well, let me tell you this." Biggs paused, and Nancy watched his back expand as he drew in a big breath.

Then Biggs leveled a finger at Ned and said, "One more slipup and you're out of a job!"

Chapter Three

NANCY BIT HER LIP. Poor Ned! He was really getting a working over.

At that moment the door to the head of the department's office opened and Joe Packard came out, briefcase in hand. Nancy had met him once or twice before. He was an imposing figure, very tall and lean, with a thick shock of white hair. He caught Nancy's eye and winked at her. Then he addressed Wally Biggs.

"Why don't you give the boy a break, Wally?" he said in a mild voice. "I think we can assume his motives were good, even if he was a little overzealous. I'm sure he won't do it again."

Wally Biggs turned around, his jowls quivering. "Yes, Joe, but I—"

"No buts, Wally," Packard said firmly. "I'm

sure Ned got the message. Now, why don't you go home? I'm sure you've had a long day."

"Right," Biggs said, trying to sound as if that were what he had been planning all along.

Nancy had to suppress a laugh. Packard had certainly taken the wind out of Biggs's sails!

Biggs caught Nancy's eye and glared at her before hurrying off.

When Biggs was out of earshot, Ned emerged from his office. "Hi," he said to Nancy in a weak voice before turning to Joe Packard.

"Thanks a million, Mr. Packard," he said. "I really appreciate your coming to my defense."

The department head set down his briefcase and leaned against a desk. "I'm glad to know you're being vigilant," he said, "although it does sound as if you may have gone overboard last night. But you're entitled to at least one mistake when you're starting out."

"It wasn't a mistake!" Ned said earnestly. "I mean, the way I handled it was wrong—I admit that. But I know I'm right about Foyle faking his claim. I reread the report today, and it just doesn't ring true."

Packard was frowning. "Foyle—Foyle," he said. He took a book of cardboard matches from his pocket, pulled off a single match and peeled the thin layers of gray cardboard into little curls. Catching Nancy staring at him, he grinned. "Habit," he told her. "I guess it's a holdover from the days when I smoked.

"Now, the Foyle claim," he resumed, raising his eyes to Ned. "You told me about that case, right? The man drove into a cement barrier, then claimed he had head injuries that would keep him from doing his job?"

Ned nodded eagerly. "Right."

Packard shrugged. "Even if you're correct in saying that this man you saw last night is the same guy who filed the claim with us—and I'm not saying you *are* right—there's probably no way to prove the extent of his injuries. Head injuries are next to impossible to verify. The guy could be out of bed, even walking around, with a mild concussion or skull fracture."

"But the medical report said he'd be out of commission for months," Ned protested. "That's why he got so much money, because he couldn't work."

"Out of commission and not able to work are two different things, aren't they?" Nancy put in.

Packard gave her an approving look. "Yes, they are, in this case. The fellow could be in some sort of job that requires a lot of reading, for example. With any kind of injury that affected his eyes, he'd be disabled as far as his work went, even if he could—say, for instance, go out to dinner. Tell me, who was the doctor who signed the claim?"

"His name is Dr. Robert Meyers," Ned replied.

Packard snapped his fingers. "There, you see? Meyers is a fine doctor. In fact, he was my wife's physician for years. Solid man. And he was willing to sign the claim. That's why I told you to agree to a settlement, if you'll remember. The man did have the accident, and the money he got from us is less than he would have gotten if we had gone to court—so don't worry about it." He bowed in Nancy's direction. "Take this lovely young lady out to dinner instead."

Nancy smiled. "Sounds good to me."

After a minute Ned shook his head. "Thanks for your concern, sir," he said. "But I can't just let it slide."

"Well, I must say I admire your persistence," Packard said with a smile. "All right, son. Go ahead and pursue this investigation if you want. Just make sure you're a little more discreet in the future."

Ned grinned. "I will, sir."

"Fine. And now I'd better say good night to you both. I'm late for an appointment," Packard said. He picked up his briefcase and strode out.

"Where should we eat?" Nancy asked when Packard was gone.

Ned didn't seem to hear her. Raking his fingers through his light brown hair, he muttered, "You heard what Wally Biggs said about me being irresponsible. Nan, the only way I'll ever get Biggs off my back is to prove to him that I was right all along."

"But Packard made it clear that he believes in you," Nancy pointed out.

Ned shook his head. "Mr. Packard is a terrific guy, but I can't let him fight my battles for me. I have to follow this up, don't you see? Will you help me?"

In a flash, Nancy saw her summer with Ned being swallowed up by this investigation.

Then she mentally kicked herself for selfishness. She thought of all the times Ned had stood by her. How could she say no to him now? And besides, she'd been complaining about how she never saw him. This was her chance to spend more time with him.

"Of course I'll help, Ned," she promised.

"You're terrific!" Ned said, breaking into a smile. Drawing Nancy into his strong arms, he planted a kiss on her lips.

"Mmmm. I'll go along with that," Nancy murmured. A pleasant shiver slid along her spine as he held her. "So what do we do first?"

Ned laughed. "Boy, it feels funny to hear you asking me that instead of the other way around. Okay, here's the plan. I want to stake out this Foyle guy's house, starting now."

"What, no dinner *again?*" Nancy complained in a teasing voice.

"I know a deli that makes great sandwiches," Ned retorted. "I'm treating." He went into his office to straighten up his desk. "I got Foyle's address off his claim form," he continued, talking over his shoulder. "I figure we'll spot him entering or leaving. Then, after we make sure it's the same guy we saw in the restaurant last night, we'll take a photograph."

"Sounds like a good start," Nancy told Ned as they walked down the stairs. "But will that prove anything? All that shows is that it's the same guy. It doesn't prove anything about his head injury either way."

"Ah! That's phase two," Ned told her. He

raised a finger to wave good night to the security guard. "I'm going to follow our friend T. N. Foyle around with my camera until I can get a shot of him doing something that he absolutely could not do with a serious head injury."

"Like what?" Nancy asked.

"Like dance. If only I'd thought of this last night! Didn't you hear Foyle and his girlfriend make plans to go dancing?"

Nancy nodded. "Sounds good to me." She thought of warning Ned that his plans would involve long hours of tracking, on top of the time he put in at work. But all she said was "Let's go!"

First they went to Kirshner's delicatessen, where Ned bought thick roast beef sandwiches and cans of soda. Then, following Ned's instructions, Nancy drove to 421 Beechwood Street, the address T. N. Foyle had listed on his claim form.

Foyle's home was in an undistinguished-looking town house on a narrow one-way street near the center of Mapleton. A few lights showed in the first-floor windows. Nancy parked under some low-hanging branches across the street.

"So tell me about this claim," she urged Ned as they ate their sandwiches.

Ned sipped his soda. "Well, according to the report, Foyle was driving at night and skidded on an oily patch on the road. The car went out of control, and he slammed into a barrier and hit his head. He managed to walk to a house to call for an ambulance. A few days later he threatened to bring a suit against Mapleton for not keeping its roads clean. His claim was that the town's negligence had caused him injuries that made it impossible to do his job—he's an accountant. Mutual Life insures the town for liability, so that's where I came in. Mr. Packard said the court costs and all would be horrendous, so we decided to offer him a settlement, which he accepted."

"Sounds pretty straightforward to me," Nancy said.

Ned went on, "The reason I'm suspicious is that Foyle's symptoms—double vision, stuff like that—didn't start until a couple of days *after* the doctor at the hospital emergency room checked him out and said he was okay. I suspect that he thought it over and decided that if he could fake symptoms, he could make a mint by suing the town for damages. Since I'm the one who investigated the claim, I feel responsible for straightening the whole mess out."

"It seems like a long shot," Nancy remarked, half to herself.

Ned didn't answer, but Nancy saw him frown and immediately felt a pang of guilt. Was she being too discouraging? Could George be right about her not wanting Ned to get involved in investigative work?

"But if anyone can solve this case, you can, Mr. Insurance Dragon," she added quickly, and was pleased that Ned smiled at her.

After a few minutes Ned got out of the car. "I'm going to ring the doorbell," he told Nancy. "If Foyle answers, I'll snap his picture. If anyone else answers, I'll ask for Foyle and see what happens."

"Be careful," Nancy called after him. She watched him cross the narrow street and go up to the door. After a moment it was answered by a thin, elderly woman. She and Ned spoke briefly before he turned around and came back to the car.

"That was Foyle's landlady," he reported. "She says she has no idea when he'll be in."

"Well, these things happen," Nancy told him. She eased her seat back to get a little more legroom. "Now I guess we just watch and wait."

Four hours later Nancy was feeling tired and grimy, and her neck was stiff from staring at the house across the street.

"Ned," she said. "It's after eleven, and I'm beat. Can we try again tomorrow?"

"Okay, okay," he said, yawning. "I guess we've done enough staking out for one day."

Giving Ned a grateful smile, Nancy started the car and drove the short distance to his house.

"I'll call you in the morning," he told her. He gave her a quick kiss and got out. "And, Nancy, remember one thing—I'm not going to give up until I prove my case."

On Saturday morning Nancy hung around the house for an hour or so, waiting for Ned's call, but it didn't come. When she tried to call him, the line was busy. At last she decided to go out and run some errands.

When she came home at two, she asked Hannah if Ned had called.

The gray-haired housekeeper looked up from the kitchen table and smiled at Nancy. "No, he hasn't," she replied. "Do you two have plans for today?"

"I thought we did," Nancy said, frowning. "He was supposed to call me this morning."

At that moment the telephone rang, and Nancy sprang for it. It was Ned, calling from what sounded like a phone booth.

"Ned, what's up? Have you been tailing Foyle?" Nancy asked.

"In a manner of speaking," Ned said. His voice was high and strained. "Foyle is dead."

"What?" Nancy nearly dropped the phone. "Ned, what's going on?"

"Foyle is dead," Ned repeated, "and I'm at the Mapleton police station—under arrest. Nancy, they think I killed him!"

Chapter Four

FOR A SECOND Nancy couldn't even breathe. Ned under arrest—for *murder?*

"Did—did I hear you right?" she croaked at last. "They think *you—*"

"Yes. I found the body and the weapon, and then the police found me." Ned's voice sounded weak and scared, and Nancy's heart went out to him.

"Oh, Ned. How horrible!"

Ned gave a shaky laugh. "Tell me about it. Listen, I'm not allowed to talk long," he hurried on. "I'll explain it all when I see you. I need your help, Nan. And I need a lawyer."

"My father," Nancy said, trying to pull her thoughts together. "I'll get my father."

"Please—come as soon as you can."

There was a catch in Ned's voice that made tears spring to Nancy's eyes. "Hang on," she said. "We'll be there in no time. And don't worry, Ned, we'll get you out of this!"

"Nancy, what's the matter?" Hannah exclaimed as Nancy hung up the phone. "You're trembling!"

Nancy wiped her eyes and took a deep breath. "It's crazy. Ned's been arrested. The Mapleton police think he killed a man," she explained hurriedly. "That's all I know. Where's Dad? Ned needs a lawyer, and Dad's the best there is."

"Oh, my goodness!" Hannah exclaimed. For a moment her normally cheerful face went slack with shock. Then all at once she collected herself. "Er—your father's at his office. He went in to do some paperwork. Is there anything I can do to help?"

Nancy was already on her way out the door. "Call Dad and tell him I'll pick him up in ten minutes. Thanks, Hannah."

Nancy made it to Carson Drew's downtown office in nine minutes flat. She could see her father standing outside the building when she arrived. With his salt-and-pepper hair and tall, straight bearing, he looked very dignified, and very worried. He jumped into the car, and Nancy quickly pulled away from the curb.

On the way to Mapleton, Nancy told her father what she knew about Toby Foyle and how determined Ned had been to prove that Foyle had committed insurance fraud. "Ned and Foyle had a fight Thursday night," she concluded. "I know that'll count against him when the police hear about it." She threw an anxious glance at her father.

Carson's face was grim, but his voice was soothing. "Let's not try to second-guess the investigation," he advised, brushing back his silver-flecked hair. "First, let's find out what the case against Ned is."

Just before three o'clock, Nancy parked across the street from Mapleton Police Headquarters. Nancy jumped out of the car and raced up the steps of the modest brick building, her father at her side.

Inside, Carson went straight to the desk sergeant. "I'm Ned Nickerson's attorney," he said crisply. He gestured at Nancy. "This is my, ah, assistant. May we see my client?"

The sergeant eyed Carson Drew, then said, "The Nickerson case, eh? Bill, get Nickerson and then take these people to the interrogation room, will you?"

A few minutes later they followed the uniformed officer named Bill down a dingy yellow corridor to a door with a reinforced-glass window set high into it. "He's all yours," the officer said to Nancy and Carson. "I'll be right outside if you need me."

Ned was sitting alone at a plain metal table, his head cradled in his arms. Nancy longed to rush forward and put her arms around him, but she knew it would look bad. After all, she was supposed to be a lawyer's assistant, not the girlfriend of the accused!

At the sound of the door closing, Ned raised his head and gave Nancy and her father a haggard smile. Nancy gasped quietly when she saw that his shirt was torn and his lower lip was swollen and crusted with dried blood.

"What happened to your lip?" she asked.

"I tripped and fell. Thanks for coming," he said. "It's nice to see some friendly faces."

Nancy and Carson sat down at the table, and Nancy leaned forward. "Ned, I already told my dad everything I know about you and Foyle. Now tell us what's going on," she urged.

"It's all so strange—it's like a bad dream," Ned said. He rubbed his hands wearily over his face, then looked at Nancy.

"I decided to stake out Foyle's house alone this morning," he explained. "I didn't want to drag you along, since you—well, since it wasn't your case."

Nancy was embarrassed. "I would have come if you'd called," she said. But she knew she *had* discouraged Ned and felt awful about it now.

"I know you would have, but let's just say I decided to go alone. I left about a quarter to nine, and this time it looked as if I'd hit the jackpot," Ned said with a wry smile. "The minute I pulled up to the house, the door opened, and who should come out but the guy from Conchita's."

"So Toby *was* T. N. Foyle," Nancy said. "You were right about that."

Ned smiled slightly. "Yeah. The sun was in my eyes, though, so I couldn't get a shot of him," he went on. "I decided to follow him and see what he was up to. He got in his car and drove to the edge of town, to the old service road that runs parallel to the interstate. There are several warehouses out there, and he parked and went into one of them."

"Weird—what was he up to?" Nancy wondered.

"That's exactly what I asked myself," said Ned. "I gave him five minutes, and then when he didn't come out, I went in to look for him.

"It was dark in there," Ned continued. "No lights were on, and after being out in the bright sunlight I couldn't see a thing. Anyway, I groped around in the dark for quite a while, trying to figure out what I'd say when I actually found the guy, and then all of a sudden I tripped over a box and fell flat on my face. That's how I got this," he added, fingering his split lip.

"Go on," Carson urged. "What happened next?"

"Well, I sort of felt around on the floor as I was trying to get up," Ned said. "My right hand closed on something metal. And then my other hand . . ." He trailed off, swallowing hard.

"Tell us," Nancy said gently.

Ned took a deep breath, and a look of horror crossed his face. "My other hand touched a—a face," he said slowly. "It was warm, but somehow I knew the person had to be dead."

Nancy shuddered. "How awful!" she whispered.

"I couldn't even yell, I was so shocked," Ned rushed on. "I jumped up and got out of there as fast as I could. It took me a couple of minutes to find my way in the dark, and I tore my shirt on a nail. Just as I ran out, a patrol car that was driving by on the service road spotted me. I was holding a crowbar in my hand—I must have picked it up after I fell."

"Mmm," Carson Drew said in a neutral voice. "I assume that was the metal object you found on the floor? And no doubt it turned out to be the murder weapon?"

Ned nodded miserably, and Nancy cast an anguished look at her father. "That means Ned's prints are all over the murder weapon!"

"I wasn't thinking about it at the time, but I guess I must have looked pretty guilty, with my torn clothes and bloody lip," Ned said. "The police officers came over, and I told them about the body inside. All I could say was 'It's Foyle—he's dead.'" Ned glanced down at his hands. "And then the officers brought me here, and a detective started asking me what I was doing at the warehouse, how I knew who the dead man was, and so on. It never occurred to me that they could seriously think I killed the guy—so I told them everything."

"You told them about the fight you and Foyle had the other night?" Nancy asked, trying to keep the anxiety out of her voice.

Ned nodded.

Carson cleared his throat. "Did the police read you your rights and offer you legal counsel before they questioned you?" he asked.

"Yes, but I turned it down," Ned told him. "I honestly didn't think I'd need a lawyer. It was stupid of me, I guess, but I just couldn't believe anyone would think I could have killed a man."

At that moment the door to the interrogation room opened, and a thin, cold-eyed man in a gray suit walked in. "I'm Detective Ken Matsuo," he announced. "Judge Birnbaum is in her chambers, so we can proceed with the arraignment, if you are ready," he said. Then, to Nancy's horror, he asked Ned to rise, and he cuffed his wrists behind him.

"What's happening?" Nancy asked her father in an undertone as they followed Ned and Matsuo down the hall.

"Ned is going to be arraigned," he told her. "That means the formal charges are going to be read before a judge. We're in luck—Lenore Birnbaum is a fair and able judge, and she knows me. I may be able to get Ned out on bail."

In the waiting area of the police station Nancy spotted Mr. and Mrs. Nickerson. Ned's father was a big, solidly handsome man. He stopped pacing when he saw Nancy and Carson, his brown eyes full of worry. Petite, sweet-faced Mrs. Nickerson sat huddled on a wooden bench, her hands clasped tightly together.

"Stay here with the Nickersons," Carson told

Nancy. "I'll handle the arraignment. We'll come back here as soon as it's over." He strode out of the station.

For the next hour Nancy sat with Ned's parents and tried to assure them that everything would be all right. It was hard, though, to sound confident. Even though *she* knew Ned was innocent, the case against him looked so black!

At four-thirty Carson walked into the police station again, accompanied by a scowling Matsuo and Ned. Nancy immediately noticed that Ned's hands were no longer cuffed. Jumping up from the bench, she ran forward with a happy cry and threw her arms around him, forgetting that she was supposed to be a legal assistant. For a full minute he hugged her tight.

"What happened?" she asked anxiously.

"Ned, are you all right?" Mr. Nickerson chimed in, moving up behind Nancy with his wife.

"I guess so." Ned gave him a halfhearted smile and his mom a quick hug. "Mr. Drew persuaded the judge to let me out on bail."

"Ned has had an unblemished record," Carson said. "And I was able to vouch for him. I let Judge Birnbaum know I believed in his innocence, and I think that swayed her."

"Dad, you're the greatest!" Nancy cried.

Matsuo broke in. "Hate to intrude," he drawled sarcastically, "but I just want you to know, Nickerson, that I'll be keeping an eye on you. If you try to leave town before the grand jury hearing on Thursday, I'll haul you in so fast it'll make your head spin. I don't like this bail business on a murder case."

"No need to threaten, Detective," Carson said. "My client isn't going anywhere." His voice was steady, but Nancy noticed that he was frowning again. As Ned and his parents hugged, Nancy pulled her father aside.

"Dad, what's the real scoop?" she asked in a low voice. "Can you win this case?"

Carson Drew shook his head. "At this point, I'd say the odds aren't good," he said heavily. "If the case does go to trial, we could be in trouble. The evidence against Ned is very damaging. If the prosecutor is worth his salt, he'll be able to convince the jury that Ned is guilty. No, Nan, I'm afraid I can't pull this one off without you. You're the detective."

"You mean—" Nancy couldn't bring herself to finish the question.

Carson put a hand on her shoulder. "Yes. We've got to find out who really killed Toby Foyle—and we've got to prove it. Otherwise, Ned could be facing life behind bars!"

Chapter Five

NANCY BIT her knuckle. She had wanted a new case, it was true, but not *this* one. The stakes were so high! What if I can't solve it? she thought, suddenly terrified. What if I don't find the real killer, and Ned has to go to jail?

Carson Drew must have seen the tension on Nancy's face, for he said gently, "Nancy, all we can do is try. And my money's on you. So is Ned's, for that matter. We talked it over on the way back here. If we work together, we can win this case."

Nancy breathed in deeply. "Thanks, Dad. Let's hope you're right. Now," she went on, straightening up determinedly, "if I'm going to investigate, I'd better get cracking. I've got only five days before the grand jury."

"That's my girl!" Carson said proudly.

Half an hour later Nancy was seated at the Nickersons' dining room table with Ned, Bess, and George. After asking Ned's permission, she had called her friends and filled them in. She knew she'd need help with the investigation, and as Carson had pointed out to Ned, it would be foolish for him to get involved. Detective Matsuo would clearly be happy for any excuse to put Ned behind bars. Besides, if Nancy ever needed her friends' support, it was now.

"All right, let's go over the basics," Nancy began briskly. "As I see it, there are a few ways we can attack this problem."

"Go, Nan!" Bess cheered.

Nancy smiled and began to tick points off on her fingers. "First, we need to find out who had both motive and opportunity to kill Toby Foyle. That means we have to find out who his friends and associates were, what they thought of him, and where they were at the time of the murder.

"Second, we need to figure out why Foyle went to the warehouse. And third, we have to determine how the killer escaped after committing the crime."

Ned suddenly sat up a little straighter. "You just jogged my memory," he said. "When I was groping around in the dark, I heard a car starting up somewhere close outside. It didn't register until now."

"Hey, we're getting somewhere already," Nancy said, pleased.

"But how can we prove to the police that there was someone else there?" George asked.

"We'll go to the warehouse and look for physical evidence," Nancy answered. "But that'll have to wait. I'm sure the area will be swarming with police for the next twenty-four hours or so. So I think we should start by interviewing Foyle's landlady. She may be able to tell us who the victim's friends were." She turned to her boyfriend. "Ned, did you get her name?"

"Mrs. Godfrey, I think," Ned replied after thinking for a moment.

Nancy stood up. "Okay. George and Bess, why don't you come with me to see Mrs. Godfrey."

"Sounds good," George said.

The girls left Ned at his house and piled into Nancy's Mustang. When they reached 421 Beechwood Street in Mapleton, Nancy parked, and they all trooped up the concrete stoop. Nancy rang the doorbell.

A minute later a gaunt-faced woman with steel gray hair done up in a tight bun opened the door. "I hope you're not reporters," she said in a disapproving voice. "I have nothing to say."

"Uh, no, we're not reporters," Nancy said, taken aback. "Actually, Mrs. Godfrey, we're detectives. My name is Nancy Drew, and these are my associates, Bess Marvin and George Fayne."

"Hmmph. Look like a bunch of teenage girls to me," the woman said, frowning. "What do you want?"

"May we come in?" Nancy asked.

Grudgingly, Mrs. Godfrey stood aside and let the girls in. They followed the landlady through the foyer and into a spotless living room with starched white curtains and carefully polished wooden furniture.

"Mrs. Godfrey, we're investigating the death of your tenant, Toby Foyle," Nancy said in a matter-of-fact voice.

The girls took seats on the sofa, and Mrs. Godfrey perched on a straight-backed chair facing them.

The lines around Mrs. Godfrey's mouth deepened. "I don't like to speak ill of the dead," she said, "but I can't say I was surprised to hear that that young man had come to a bad end. He was a sly one. But you're wasting your time investigating. The police told me they already caught the boy who did it—said it's the same young man who came here last night looking for Mr. Foyle." The landlady shook her head. "I never would have pegged him for a criminal."

"He isn't one!" Bess burst out. "Ned didn't do it!"

Mrs. Godfrey gave the girls a questioning look. "So you know the boy?"

"Yes, we do," Nancy admitted. She hadn't wanted to tell Mrs. Godfrey about her connection with Ned, but now that the story was out, she saw no point in denying it. "And we know Ned didn't kill Toby. But we have to prove that to the police."

Suddenly Mrs. Godfrey's face softened. "I

liked the look of that boy when he came to the door last night. If I can help, I will."

"Oh, thank you!" Nancy cried.

"What do you want to know?" asked Mrs. Godfrey.

"First of all," Nancy said, leaning forward, "tell us what you know about Toby Foyle. How long did he live here? Where did he work? What did you think of him?"

"Who were his friends?" George put in.

"Well—" Mrs. Godfrey pursed her lips. "Mr. Foyle moved in about six months ago. He rented the rooms on the top floor. That suite has no kitchen, but it does have a private bath, and he said that was all he needed. I'd let you see it, only the police were here this morning and sealed the whole floor off."

Nancy was disappointed. She had hoped she might be able to look around Foyle's apartment for clues, but she couldn't ask Mrs. Godfrey to break the police seal.

"As for working," Mrs. Godfrey was saying, "I don't believe Mr. Foyle had a steady job—I didn't ask, since I'm not one to pry—but he always paid the rent on time. He kept very odd hours, though, no routine. A couple of times when I cleaned his rooms—that was part of our agreement, that I would clean for him—I found racing forms."

"I suspect he didn't make his money working as an accountant," Nancy murmured.

"He had to have lied about his job," George said.

Bess nodded her agreement. "Please go on," she told the landlady.

"He didn't have many friends that I know of," Mrs. Godfrey announced. "Few people ever called or visited, except for that girlfriend of his, Michelle Ferraro." Mrs. Godfrey shook her head disapprovingly. "She was as bad as a whole army, though. Why, she would call here four or five times a day. I finally had to ask Mr. Foyle to get a phone installed. He got it in just last week."

"Michelle Ferraro." Nancy thought of the blond girl who had been in Conchita's with Foyle. Could that have been Michelle? "Do you have her phone number, by any chance?" she asked.

"No, but it's probably in the book. She lives over in West Mapleton, I believe."

"Well, thank you very much for talking with us, Mrs. Godfrey," Nancy said. She rose to go, then paused because she had almost forgotten to ask the most important question. "Just one last question—did Mr. Foyle seem in good health to you during the past month?"

"In good health?" Mrs. Godfrey seemed surprised. "Yes, he seemed fine. Why?"

Nancy explained about Foyle's insurance claim. As she talked, Mrs. Godfrey's lips pressed into an even thinner line.

"There wasn't a thing wrong with him," she declared when Nancy was finished. "He was just plain lying, that's all. I always suspected the man was a scoundrel, and this just proves it."

Nancy gave Mrs. Godfrey her telephone number in River Heights, just in case the landlady remembered anything more. Then she and her friends said goodbye.

"Nan, do you think that insurance claim is important to your investigation?"

Nancy shrugged. "Definitely indirectly, because it proves what kind of character Foyle was. Possibly directly—how it ties in I don't exactly know yet. One thing is clear to me, though. Foyle *did* fake the insurance claim, and he knew that Ned knew about it. He was really scared that night at Conchita's. At the time I thought it was because he was afraid Ned might hit him, but now I think it was because he realized Ned had found him out." She steered into a left turn, then bit her thumbnail thoughtfully.

"It's possible that he had an accomplice in this scheme. His girlfriend, maybe—or more likely, the doctor who signed the claim. And it's also possible that the accomplice killed him to keep him from panicking and blowing the whole scam."

"Wow! Good thinking!" George said, leaning forward from the back seat. "So now I guess we have to check out this Michelle, as well as the doctor who signed the claim form."

"Exactly." Nancy parked in front of Ned's house, and the girls went inside. While Bess and George told Ned about their talk with Mrs. Godfrey, Nancy looked up Michelle Ferraro's address and phone number. She dialed, but there was no answer.

By now it was almost seven o'clock, and Mrs. Nickerson invited the three girls to stay for dinner. Bess and George were expected home, so they took off in George's car, but Nancy stayed. She had a feeling Ned needed her right then. He looked pale and worn. The Nickersons' phone had been ringing all afternoon with reporters from the local papers trying to get statements from Ned or his parents.

Conversation at the dinner table was strained. No one really wanted to talk about the charges that were hanging over Ned's head, but it seemed false and trivial to talk about anything else. Finally Nancy and Ned excused themselves and went out to sit on the swing on the front porch.

The evening was warm. The air was filled with the scent of flowers, and the light from the windows made little pools of illumination in the heavily shaded yard.

Ned drew in a deep breath. "On a night like tonight, it's hard to believe any of this is really happening," he said sadly.

"I know." Nancy put her hand in his. "I promised your mom and dad that we'd get you off, and I won't let any of you down. We'll solve this case one way or another."

"Have I told you lately how great you are?" Ned asked with a tender smile. "I do love you, Nan—and I have faith in you." Rising, he pulled her up and into his arms. They stood that way for a long moment, just enjoying the warmth of being close.

Nancy turned her head as she heard a faint rustling noise in the grass beside the porch. "What's that?" she asked, peering into the darkness.

Suddenly a black, hunched shape loomed up out of the shadows. Nancy gasped. And then the night exploded in fierce white light.

Chapter Six

NANCY DUCKED INSTINCTIVELY, pulling Ned down with her. Green and orange afterimages danced in front of her eyes.

"What was that?" Ned cried.

"That was a primo shot to go with my article in tomorrow's paper," came a familiar voice.

"Brenda Carlton," Nancy muttered. Now her vision was beginning to clear, and she could see the outlines of the teenage reporter's face as the tall, dark-haired girl approached.

Brenda wrote for a River Heights paper called *Today's Times,* which was conveniently owned by her father, Frazier Carlton. The young reporter was a frequent thorn in Nancy's side. Her competitive nature drove her to meddle whenever she could in order to get a hot scoop. In the past her interference had almost blown several of Nancy's cases.

Brenda pushed back her dark hair and smiled triumphantly. "Yes, it's me—in the flesh," she purred. "Now, what should my caption be? 'Teen Sleuth Gets Friendly with Murder Suspect'? Or maybe 'Sleuth Nancy Drew and Murder Suspect Ned Nickerson: Could a Crowbar Pry These Two Apart?' "

"I ought to rip the film right out of your camera," Ned said angrily.

Brenda tossed her head and said, "What a splash this'll make! All the other reporters just got the bare details off the police band radio. But I tried harder—and now I've got a terrific photograph of the prime suspect! Just wait until you see the paper tomorrow."

Nancy could imagine the trashy, sensational story Brenda would write. An article like that could permanently damage Ned's reputation, even if Nancy did manage to solve the case eventually. She *had* to talk Brenda out of it.

"Brenda," she said, "you know Ned. You know he didn't kill that man. But your article could really hurt him. Give us a break, will you?"

"I'm a reporter," Brenda said haughtily. "I tell the facts the way I see them."

"When it suits your style," Ned muttered, but Nancy put a hand on his arm. This was no time to antagonize Brenda.

"Listen," Nancy said, trying a different tactic.

"You're a smart girl, Brenda. You and I both know that Ned is innocent. So why not use that?"

"What do you mean?" Brenda asked, her voice suspicious.

"I'm offering you a scoop to end all scoops," Nancy said quickly. "I'm going to track down the real killer—and I promise that when I do, you'll get the exclusive story. That is, if *you* promise not to write any stories about Ned before then. How about it—is it a deal?"

Brenda was silent for a moment. "How do I know you'll call me?" she asked at last.

Rolling her eyes, Nancy said, "You'll have to trust me. I give you my word of honor."

After another long pause Brenda said, "Okay. I'll be waiting to hear from you. And you'd better call me soon, Nancy Drew." With that, Brenda flounced off to her car.

"Thanks," said Ned, breathing a sigh of relief. "That was some fast talking you did, Nancy."

"Right," Nancy replied. She didn't add what she was thinking—all the fast talking in the world wouldn't help Ned, unless she delivered on her promise and caught the real criminal!

The next day Nancy got up early. She went out and bought copies of the Mapleton papers, which she brought home to read along with the River Heights papers. She was a little cheered to see that, although Foyle's murder had made the front pages, a bureaucratic scandal in Chicago had stolen the headlines. The pieces on Foyle's murder were short and not very detailed. Still, Ned's high-school yearbook picture did appear in two of the articles, and his name was mentioned in all of them.

Nancy decided not to call on Bess and George to help that day. She wanted to track down suspects, and she preferred to do that by herself. A gang of girls wouldn't put a reluctant talker at ease.

By ten-thirty, Nancy was on the road to Mapleton. She had already called Ned and gotten the name and home address of the doctor who had signed the medical report for Toby Foyle's false claim. Foyle had gone to Dr. Robert Meyers three days *after* his accident, Nancy recalled. That was pretty suspicious. The question was, had the doctor been an innocent dupe in Foyle's insurance scam, or was he a participant?

Dr. Meyers lived in a pleasant, prosperous-looking neighborhood near the center of Mapleton. His house was only two blocks from 421 Beechwood, where Toby Foyle had lived, Nancy noted. She wondered if that fact had any significance.

A moment after she rang the bell, the oak front door of Dr. Meyers's house swung open to reveal a plump, pink-faced man with a fringe of gray hair around a shiny scalp.

"Dr. Meyers?" Nancy inquired politely. At his nod, she went on, "My name is Nancy Drew. I'd like to talk to you about one of your patients—Toby Foyle."

At the name the twinkle in Dr. Meyers's blue

eyes faded, and his expression became serious. "Oh, yes, poor man," he said. "I just read about his death in the paper. Shocking—and to think the killer is a local boy! What a tragedy. Come in, come in."

Meyers led Nancy through the house and into a small, sunny backyard with a patio and wrought-iron garden furniture. He waved her to a seat and took one himself. "Now, how did you know Toby Foyle?" he asked curiously.

"Actually, I didn't know him," Nancy said. "I'm a private investigator. I'm looking into his death, and I'm also interested in some—inconsistencies in his medical history."

Meyers drew back, looking a little offended. "Inconsistencies—such as—" he prompted.

Nancy explained Ned's theory about Foyle having falsified his insurance claim. When she had finished, Dr. Meyers shook his head.

"I really shouldn't be discussing a patient with you, Ms. Drew," he said. "But I suppose in this case it's acceptable. As for Mr. Foyle having falsified his trauma symptoms, it's my opinion that he did not. Otherwise I would never have signed his claim! It's difficult to verify these things, though," Meyers went on. "He had a bruise or two—no detectable damage to the skull, according to my colleague at the hospital emergency room. But you can certainly have a head injury without a fractured skull. I can say that when I examined his eyes, his pupils were not contracting properly. He also complained of frequent headaches and double vision."

"I see. Thank you, Dr. Meyers. You've been very helpful," Nancy said. She gave the doctor her sunniest smile. "If I could just ask you one more question?"

Meyers smiled back. "Of course, my dear."

Still smiling, Nancy leaned forward in her chair. She had to be alert for the tiniest suspicious reaction on Meyers's part. So far he hadn't betrayed any nervousness or worry, but the next question ought to shake him up a bit.

"Where were you yesterday morning between the hours of nine and ten?" she asked softly.

Meyers blinked. Then, as he realized what she was asking, his face flushed with anger. "Are you implying that *I* might have killed Toby Foyle?" he demanded. "That's absurd! Young lady, I'm a doctor. I preserve life, I don't destroy it! Anyway, the police have already arrested the killer. It's an open-and-shut case.

"However, if you really want to know, I have office hours on Saturday mornings. Yesterday I had a full roster of patients. The first one arrived at eight-thirty, and the last one didn't leave until well after one in the afternoon. I didn't leave my office at any time during that period."

Nancy nodded. If Dr. Meyers was lying, it would be easy to find out by asking his receptionist, or checking with his patients from that day. But he sounded very sure of himself.

She rose to go. "Thank you again," she said to the plump doctor. "I'm sorry if I seemed rude. It's just that I don't have much time. An innocent guy will go to jail if I don't find out who really killed Toby Foyle."

Meyers cleared his throat. "Well, then, I suppose I understand. No harm done."

After he had shown her out, Nancy walked slowly to her car, thinking hard.

Maybe her accomplice theory was no good. Meyers, a doctor, was the most obvious choice of partner for a scam involving medical insurance. But it looked as if he couldn't have killed Foyle—though she still had to check his alibi, of course. If he was telling the truth, then perhaps Foyle's death had nothing to do with the insurance scam.

On the other hand, maybe the accomplice in the scam was someone other than Meyers, and *that* person and Foyle could have had a falling out. . . .

Nancy sighed. All her speculating was useless without some solid leads and evidence.

After climbing into her Mustang, Nancy took out her notebook and studied the address she had written down for Michelle Ferraro in West Mapleton. "You're next, Michelle," she said out loud. "I hope you give me a lead."

The building where Michelle lived turned out to be a dilapidated three-story structure with rickety wooden stairs running up the outside of the building to the apartments. Nancy scanned the rows of mailboxes on the breezeway wall until she found the name Ferraro. Michelle lived on the third floor in the rear of the building.

Nancy climbed the two flights of stairs to

apartment 3-R and knocked on the door. She could hear loud, pulsing rock music coming from inside. No one answered, so after a minute Nancy knocked again, harder.

The music suddenly stopped, and a girl's voice called, "Yeah, I'm coming. Hold on."

In another minute the door flew open, and Nancy found herself facing a young woman of about twenty-three, with masses of brunette hair held back from her face by a leopard-print scarf. She wore a short, flounced skirt with leggings underneath. In her right hand she held a paring knife.

"Hi. Is Michelle Ferraro here?" Nancy asked, eyeing the knife a little nervously.

The girl scowled. "I'm Michelle."

Nancy was startled. This definitely wasn't the blond girl she'd seen Foyle with at Conchita's. Could there be two Michelle Ferraros in West Mapleton? Or had Foyle been out with another girl that night? There was only one way to find out.

"Uh—I wanted to talk to you about Toby Foyle," she began. But she got no further.

"So *you're* the one he was dating. Why, you little witch!" Michelle snarled. "I can't believe you've got the nerve to show up here." Her eyes narrowed. "I ought to teach you a lesson."

Michelle raised her hand, and Nancy saw a sudden glint of silver. Then Michelle lunged straight at her!

Chapter Seven

Nancy's detective instincts took over as she saw Michelle come at her with the knife. She jumped to one side, turning in midair so that her back was against the wooden rail of the landing. Then, as Michelle hurtled past her, she grabbed the girl's arm and twisted it up behind her back.

Michelle gave a cry of pain. The knife dropped from her fingers, and Nancy kicked it off the edge of the landing. It skittered down the stairs, out of sight.

Now that the danger was past, Nancy's knees turned to water. That had been close!

"Let me go!" Michelle panted, struggling.

"I don't know what you think you're doing," Nancy said angrily. "But attacking a person with a knife is really dumb—especially when that person is a detective looking into a murder case!"

Michelle abruptly stopped struggling. "You—you're a detective?" she asked in a shocked voice.

"That's right. My name's Nancy Drew. I'm investigating the death of Toby Foyle. Maybe I should call the police in to talk to you."

"No! Look, I didn't mean to hurt you, not really. I had the knife in my hand because I was opening some boxes with it, and I forgot I had it. That's the truth, I swear!" Michelle took a deep breath and went on in a calmer voice. "I thought you were someone else. I'm sorry—I was mad, that's all."

I wonder what she does when she's really furious? Nancy wondered. From the comment Michelle had made when she first opened the door, it sounded as though she thought Nancy was the "other woman." Maybe Toby had been two-timing her, and Michelle had found out. Was that a motive for murder?

Nancy released Michelle's arm, watching the girl warily. But all Michelle did was rub her wrist and look sulky.

"So who *did* you think I was?" Nancy asked in a conversational tone.

Michelle dropped her gaze to the floor. "No one. I mean, it has nothing to do with your investigation. Look, I don't understand why you're here. I thought they already know who did it. That's what the papers said."

"They haven't proved anything yet," Nancy said. Then she had an idea. Michelle might be willing to tell her a lot more if Nancy made her think she wasn't a suspect in the murder.

"In fact, I'm helping the prosecution put its case together," Nancy fibbed. "I'm trying to eliminate all the surprises—you know, make sure the defense doesn't come up with any witnesses or facts that we can't account for."

Michelle nodded slowly. "I see," she said.

"May I come in?" Nancy asked her.

Michelle moved aside and gestured for Nancy to go into the apartment. Nancy stepped through the door and looked around.

The place was messy and cramped. A huge, apparently new home entertainment center dominated one wall: the teak cabinet held a big color television set, a VCR, and expensive-looking stereo equipment, including a compact disk player and a cassette deck. On the floor lay two speakers, which had obviously just come out of their shipping boxes. Shreds of brown cardboard from the boxes littered the carpet.

I wonder where Michelle got the money to pay for all this stuff? Nancy thought.

"So what do you want to know?" Michelle asked.

Nancy pulled out a spiral pad and pen. "I've already got your name and address. Just let me jot down your employer's name and a number where we can reach you during the day if we need to," she said briskly.

"I'm a salesperson at Karsh's," she said. She gave Nancy the switchboard number.

Nancy knew that Karsh's was a local department store. She also knew that salespeople didn't generally make enough money to buy lots of expensive stereo equipment all at once. Her interest was piqued. She'd have to follow this up. If Michelle had some unexplained income, that could point to her being Foyle's accomplice in the insurance scam!

Nancy took a seat. "Okay. Now, start by telling me how well you knew Mr. Foyle," she said. "I understand you dated?"

"Yes, that's right." Michelle twined her fingers in her leopard-print scarf. "But I, uh—I broke up with him a few days ago. He was, uh—kind of boring. I mean, he was nice, but . . ." She trailed off.

"I know what you mean," Nancy said with a bubbly laugh. But she was thinking, That's a lie. When she'd seen Toby Foyle in Conchita's on Thursday, he hadn't looked like a guy who'd just been dumped. He'd appeared to be having a good time with the blond girl, whoever she was. Also, from what Mrs. Godfrey had said about Michelle calling several times a day, she doubted the girl had really been bored with Foyle.

No, I don't think Michelle dumped Toby, Nancy mused. If anything, Toby dumped *her* for the blond girl. That would certainly fit the theory about Michelle wanting revenge.

Nancy pretended to make some notes, then paused and said casually, "Now, I'd just like to ask about your whereabouts on Saturday morning."

Michelle's eyes narrowed in suspicion. "Why would that matter to you?" she challenged.

"Oh, believe me, I'm not accusing you of anything," Nancy said quickly. "We're only trying to make sure that there are no other possible suspects. We don't want the defense to try to cloud the issue at the trial, you see."

"Hmmm," Michelle said. She didn't seem convinced. "Well, since you ask, I got up early and went into Chicago to do some shopping. I was out until about three o'clock."

"I see." That was no alibi. Nancy made some more notes on her pad. "I'm sure we can verify that with store owners in Chicago if we need to. I just have one more question, if it's okay with you. Mr. Foyle was recently in a car accident, as I'm sure you know. He received some money in compensation for his injuries. Now, my question is—"

Nancy was interrupted by an angry exclamation from Michelle. "What injuries?" she said. "He came out of that accident without a scratch. And what money? He sure didn't spend any of it on me."

"I see." Nancy scribbled some more. Her thoughts were racing. Michelle's outburst had sounded honest—unlike most of the other things she'd said. If that was so, Michelle hadn't known about Foyle's insurance scam. She could still be the murderer, Nancy realized. But if she was, her motive was jealousy and had nothing to do with the scam.

Of course, there was still the blond girl to consider. Maybe she had worked with Foyle to fake the insurance claim. Nancy let out a sigh of frustration. Unless I get some leads on who this mysterious blonde is, she thought, I'm batting zero on the accomplice theory.

"Thanks for your help," Nancy said, getting up. "May I call you if I have any more questions?"

"Sure," Michelle drawled. She seemed skeptical as she added, "Good luck on your case."

As Nancy got into her Mustang, she saw Michelle at the window of her apartment, twisting her fingers in her scarf and staring down at the car.

Nancy drove away, wondering. Michelle had no alibi for the time of the murder, and Nancy was sure she'd had a grudge against Toby Foyle. Nancy herself had been a victim of Michelle's murderous temper. If she could find some physical evidence to connect the girl to the scene of the crime, she'd have the makings of a real case. It bothered her a little that this solution seemed to have nothing to do with the insurance scam, but Michelle certainly was a strong suspect so far.

It was early afternoon, so Nancy decided to drop by Ned's house to bring him up to date. When she arrived, she was surprised to find Joe Packard sitting in the den with Ned.

"Mr. Packard believes I'm innocent," Ned announced, obviously pleased.

Packard's face was full of concern as he greeted Nancy. "I came over to offer my support. I read about the arrest this morning, and I knew right away the police were barking up the wrong tree," he told her. "Ned couldn't have killed that fellow—it's not in him. I'm glad to hear your father's representing him, Nancy. Carson Drew has an unbeatable reputation as a defense lawyer."

"That's not all I've got going for me," Ned told Packard. He put his arm around Nancy and said proudly, "Nancy here is the best detective there is, and she's going to find out for us who killed Foyle."

"Terrific!" Packard exclaimed. "Have you started investigating yet?"

"Yes, I have," Nancy said.

"What's the scoop?" Ned asked eagerly.

Quickly Nancy told him about her interviews with Dr. Meyers and Michelle, including her theory that Michelle might have killed Foyle in revenge for breaking up with her.

"I'm not altogether crazy about the idea," she added, frowning. "There's no clear connection between her and the insurance scam, but she certainly seems violent enough. I mean, she came after me with a knife just because she thought I *might* be the girl who'd stolen her boyfriend!"

Ned scowled. "I wish you'd let me come with you," he said, his voice filled with concern. "I don't like you endangering yourself. You could have been badly hurt!"

"I wasn't, though," Nancy said, hugging him. "Anyway, you're definitely worth the risk. But listen, before I go making any accusations, there's one more possible accomplice I'd like to track down—the blond girl we saw with Foyle at Conchita's. Think hard, Ned. Do you have any idea who she is?"

Ned scrunched up his face in thought, then shook his head. "No, I know I've seen her somewhere, but I just can't think where," he confessed. "I'll keep trying to remember."

Packard was peeling a match, a thoughtful look on his face. "It sounds as if you're on the right trail, Nancy," he said. "This Michelle Ferraro sounds capable of murder, but I also must say I agree with Ned—you're taking big risks. Be careful."

"I will, Mr. Packard," Nancy replied.

"Good. Well, I ought to be going," Packard said, getting to his feet. "Ned, if there's any way I can help out, or even if you just want to talk, please don't hesitate to call on me. You know, I'm right in the neighborhood."

"Thanks, Mr. Packard." Ned cleared his throat awkwardly, then held out his hand. Packard shook it. "I really appreciate your support, sir. It means a lot to me."

"Forget it, son." With a wink and a smile, Packard was gone.

"It was nice of him to come by," Nancy remarked.

Ned grinned. "Yeah, wasn't it? You know, between Mr. Packard's visit and the great news about your new lead, I'm beginning to feel as if I have a chance. I feel like celebrating!"

Nancy wasn't so sure how solid her leads were, but she was pleased to see Ned acting happier.

"Want to order in a pizza?" she suggested. "I could do with some lunch."

Ned scooped up her car keys and jingled them. "Let's go out. I haven't left the house since I got home from the police station yesterday. I could use a change of scene."

"I don't think that's a good idea," Nancy warned. "What if you're spotted by reporters? Maybe you should just lie low for a while."

"Don't worry." Ned waved a hand. "No one's been bothering me today. The phone's hardly rung at all, and only one reporter came to the door. The story in Chicago must be keeping them all busy."

Nancy shrugged. She didn't have the heart to dampen his spirits. "Okay, then," she said with a smile. "If you really want to go out, let's go."

"Great!" He was already loping out the door to the car, and Nancy had to run to catch up.

"So what's your next move?" asked Ned as they drove toward Mama's, a pizza place on the outskirts of Mapleton.

"I'm going out to the warehouse tonight," Nancy replied, her eyes on the road. "I want to see if I can find any hard clues there. There's a chance the police might have missed something."

"Will you take Bess and George with you for protection?" Ned asked.

Nancy pulled into a parking spot in Mama's lot, and they got out. "Yes," she agreed. "Please don't worry about me."

Inside the little restaurant a group of nine or ten teenagers sat at a long table next to the wall, and a plump, dark-haired woman was bustling around serving them sodas. Most of the other tables had only one or two people at them. A sign by the cash register read, Please Wait to Be Seated.

They waited. As they stood there, Nancy noticed that one of the teenagers was staring hard at Ned. He nudged the girl next to him and whispered something in her ear. When the girl started staring at Ned, too, Nancy began to feel a little nervous. Had they recognized him from his picture in the papers?

"Is everyone staring at us?" Ned murmured. He was starting to be uncomfortable.

They didn't have to wait long for the answer to Ned's question. Above the low hum of conversation in the restaurant, an angry muttering started at the table. Then, all of a sudden, the guy who'd first noticed Ned stood up.

"Hey!" he shouted. "Get out of here! We don't want any murderers in here!"

Chapter Eight

DEAD SILENCE FELL instantly over the little restaurant. The gaze of every single patron snapped to Ned's face.

Nancy's heart sank right to her toes. Glancing up at Ned, she saw that his face had gone completely white. Grabbing his hand, she pulled him toward the door. "Let's go," she murmured. "We don't need any more trouble than we've already got."

Outside, Ned walked to the car like a robot. He climbed in and sat staring blankly ahead of him. After getting in on the driver's side, Nancy put her hand over his. "Ned, it was just an ignorant comment," she said, trying to comfort him. "The law says you're innocent until proven guilty, and

I'm sure everyone else in this town remembers that."

"I know that guy," Ned said quietly. "That was Denny Goldman. He was in my class in high school."

"Oh, Ned. I'm so sorry." Nancy didn't know what else to say. She could only imagine how horrible he must feel, having people he knew condemn him in public.

"Nancy, he thinks I did it!" Ned burst out suddenly. "How many other people think the same thing? How many of my friends are going to turn the other way the next time they see me on the street? Even if I don't get sent to prison, everyone will always remember that I was accused of murder. What's the rest of my life going to be like?"

"Stop it!" Nancy said in a firm voice. "The rest of your life is going to be just fine. Know why? Because I'm going to find out who really killed Toby Foyle. I'm going to find out *before* the grand jury hearing on Thursday. Before you ever have to walk into that courtroom, I'll have evidence that will convince the prosecutor to drop the charges. Then Brenda Carlton will write the splashiest story you've ever read, and everyone will know the truth—that you're *innocent.* And that's a promise, Ned Nickerson."

"Whoa!" Ned held up his hands, a faint grin on his face. "Okay, Nan, I get the message. Thanks for the pep talk. I really needed it. But let's just go home, okay? I see now that you were right—I *should* keep out of sight until this thing is over. Let's go home and make some sandwiches."

Nancy started the car. "I'll make you another promise," she said, smiling. "When it is over, I'll take you to Mama's for a victory pizza with the works. Deal?"

Ned laughed out loud. "Deal!"

That evening over dinner Nancy updated her father on the investigation. She didn't tell him about her plan to sneak into the warehouse with Bess and George that night. She thought it would be better if he didn't know, since what she was planning to do wasn't exactly legal. It would look bad for Carson, as Ned's lawyer, to be involved in any kind of shady investigating. Besides, she knew it would only make him worry.

Instead, Nancy told her father that she was going over to George's house. She'd called both George and Bess earlier and made plans to meet them.

They were waiting on the porch when she drove up in her Mustang at eight o'clock. Both wore jeans, sneakers, and dark blouses as Nancy had instructed. They hurried to the car.

"Let's go," George said, strapping her long, lean frame into the front passenger seat. Her brown eyes sparkled with excitement. "I hope we find some good clues."

"Do you really think this girl Michelle is the one who killed Toby Foyle?" Bess asked from the back seat. She leaned forward, looping her arms around George's headrest.

Nancy pursed her lips. "Let's say she's the most likely suspect I've got at the moment. I'm pretty sure Foyle was cheating on her and she found out. She's got a really violent temper—and she has no alibi. On top of that, she seems to have a lot more money than she should have. She has all this brand-new, expensive stereo stuff in her apartment."

"I don't see what the money question has to do with this case," George put in. "I thought you decided she wasn't involved in the insurance scam with Foyle."

Nancy nodded. "You're right. If she killed Foyle, money wasn't the issue. It just struck me as odd, that's all, a salesgirl having so many new, costly things. It doesn't add up."

They drove in silence until they reached the service road on the outskirts of Mapleton, where the warehouses were. The area was dark and deserted. The byroad seemed to be seldom used, and there were no streetlights.

Nancy steered into the graveled parking area in front of a warehouse that was surrounded by sawhorses. Her headlights shone on stenciled letters on the sawhorses.

" 'Police line—do not cross.' This must be the place," George said with a nervous laugh.

Nancy parked in front of the sawhorses and the three girls got out. Nancy cocked her head, listening for the sound of approaching cars, but the night was still. She surveyed the big building. A strip of yellow tape that said "Crime Scene" was stretched across the front door. The three girls circled the warehouse, looking for a way to get inside.

"The doors are all pretty well sealed," she commented. "Let's see if we can find a window."

The windows were too high for the girls to use, but finally Bess spotted a ventilation duct about six feet off the ground on the front of the building. "Will this do?" she called.

"I think so," Nancy said after inspecting it. "Good work, Bess." She dragged one of the sawhorses over, climbed up on it, and worked the grate over the duct free with her fingers.

"Uh, I don't think I'll fit through that hole," Bess said, her voice nervous. "Maybe I'd better wait out here for you guys."

Nancy laughed. "Of course you'll fit, Bess. You're as thin as I am. But if you want to stay out here, that's fine. It would probably be a good idea to have someone on guard, anyway. Here, take my car keys. If you hear anyone coming, move the Mustang out of sight."

"Sure," Bess agreed, looking relieved.

Taking the flashlight from Bess, Nancy shinnied up and crawled through the duct, then dropped to the floor inside the warehouse. Behind her, George landed with a grunt. Nancy switched on the flashlight and gazed around. Rows of metal shelving, piled high with boxes, stretched into the shadows at the far end of the cavernous building. More boxes were stacked untidily on the floor.

"What are we looking for?" George asked.

"First let's check out all the exits. I want to see how the killer got away," Nancy replied.

Together the two girls walked the length of the building. Nancy noted that there were two loading bays on one of the side walls, but they were both closed up. It would have been impossible for any one person to open the massive doors without someone to help him or her.

"What do they keep in here?" George wanted to know. "All I see is cardboard boxes with names and dates stenciled on them."

"Ned said a lot of companies store their old records here," Nancy answered. Then she snapped her fingers. "Hey—I'm glad you brought that up, George. We should try to get a list of all the companies that have storage space here. The killer probably had access to the keys to this place, since Ned said the door was unlocked when he followed Foyle inside. If we can make a match between one of the companies and any of the people involved in this case, we're in business."

"Sounds reasonable. Bess and I can work on that angle tomorrow," George offered.

"Great. Hey, look at that!" The two girls had worked their way around to the rear wall of the warehouse, and Nancy was pointing to a small door set in one corner. It opened by means of a crash bar, she saw. When the bar was pushed, the latch slid up. Nancy knew from their survey of the building that there was no handle or keyhole to open this door from the outside.

"This is it!" she said excitedly. "This is how the killer got out."

"So what does that tell us?" George asked.

"Not much," Nancy had to admit. "But at least we can show the police that someone *could* have left this way."

Next, Nancy and George inspected the aisles, going back and forth from left to right. Nancy was looking for the chalk outline the police would have drawn to mark where Foyle's body had lain. She shivered just thinking about it. It was definitely a grisly search.

They found it near the back of the warehouse. "Ugh, this is creepy," George said when she saw the chalk marks.

"I know," Nancy agreed. "We'll get out of here in a minute. Let's just look around quickly. Maybe the police missed something."

That didn't seem likely, though. As Nancy shone the flashlight over the site, she saw that it had been swept clean. It looked as if the police had picked up every last speck of dust in their search for evidence.

Nancy stepped back and nearly tripped over something solid. Turning, she saw a brown cardboard box on the floor. "This must be the box Ned tripped over," she said, shining her flashlight on it.

It had evidently been opened by the police, for the tape that covered its seams was slit and there were little brown and gray shreds of cardboard on the floor around it. The contents, which appeared to be old receipts from a clothing boutique, were untouched.

Disappointed, Nancy turned to George. "There's nothing here. The police got whatever evidence there was, I guess. Come on, let's go."

"All right." George sounded relieved.

On the way out Nancy climbed up to the duct first. She was just about to push herself through to make the leap down to the ground, when a bright light caught her in the eyes, momentarily blinding her. She froze.

Then the lights slid past Nancy, and she let out the breath she had been holding. She peeked out from the duct, waiting for her vision to clear.

When it did, she wished it hadn't. Because the first thing she saw was a black and white state police car. It was pulling into the graveled yard—and its headlights were trained directly on Bess!

Chapter Nine

LOOKING OUT through the duct, Nancy saw Bess standing by the driver's-side door of the Mustang. Her face looked stark white in the harsh glare from the cruiser's headlights, and she was obviously terrified. Nancy's heart sank. Things could be pretty sticky if Bess acted suspicious and the police started searching the area.

"What's up?" George asked from behind her.

"Shhh!" Nancy whispered. "We've got company."

She watched as two uniformed officers got out of the patrol car and approached Bess. The taller of them said, "This is an off-limits area, miss. I have to ask what you're doing here."

"Oh—officers," Bess began in a quavering

voice. Then she put on a big smile. "I'm so glad you came along! Otherwise I might have been stuck here all night."

All night? What was Bess up to? Nancy wondered.

"You see," said Bess, "I was on my way home from my friend Sally's house—she just moved here from River Heights, into the cutest little apartment. I forget the name of the street, but it's right near here. Anyway, I got onto this weird side road instead of the highway. And then my engine started making these noises, like *ping-ping*. So I pulled in here, because I was scared something was wrong and the car might blow up." She paused for a breath and Nancy stifled a giggle.

"Nothing happened, though," Bess hurried on. "So then I figured I would look under the hood and see if there were any loose screws or anything like that, so I got out of the car and shut the door—only I left the keys inside." She pointed through the car window, and Nancy saw the officers bend down to peer inside.

"But when I tried to open the door again, it was locked!" Bess concluded with a big sigh. "I swear, I can be so dumb sometimes! Do you think you could help me get my keys out?"

"Ah—certainly, miss," the taller policeman said.

The shorter officer went back to the patrol car and got a thin metal slat. He slid it down between the window and the insulating strip on Nancy's car, then struggled to unlatch the lock. A moment later the door was open. After thanking them profusely, Bess climbed in. Then, with a jaunty wave of her hand, she started the engine and drove away. The two officers looked after her, and Nancy saw the shorter one shake his head. Then they, too, drove away.

When Nancy was sure they were gone, she signaled to George that the coast was clear, then crawled the rest of the way out of the duct. George followed. After they were safely on the ground, Nancy told her about Bess's performance. They were still giggling when Bess came back to pick them up five minutes later.

"Way to go," George told her cousin. "How did you manage to pull that story off?"

"Well, when I saw the police car, I was totally scared," Bess told them. "They had already seen me, so I couldn't move the car. But then I remembered I had Nan's keys, so I opened the door a crack, tossed the keys in, and then I locked the door. I did it all with my back to them, so they'd think I was struggling to open the door."

"You were fantastic, Bess!" Nancy exclaimed as they drove away from the warehouse. "You fooled them completely!"

"I know. I felt bad about lying, though," Bess said with a sigh. "The tall one was kind of cute, you know. He had the sweetest brown eyes."

"Bess!" Nancy and George shrieked in unison. Then the three of them burst out laughing.

* * *

The phone rang soon after Nancy got up on Monday morning. It was Ned, and his voice vibrated with excitement over the phone.

"Nan, I remembered where I've seen that blond girl before—the one who was with Toby Foyle in Conchita's," he said. "She works in the accounting department at Mutual Life!"

"You're kidding!" Nancy exclaimed.

"No. I didn't make the connection because I've only seen her at work, and she looks different from the way she did at the restaurant," Ned explained. "She wears sensible suits, glasses, and no makeup. I guess she's one of those people who likes to keep her work life separate from her play life."

"Could be," Nancy agreed. Her mind was racing as she thought of the possibilities Ned's bit of news opened up. "Listen, if she works at Mutual Life, she'd have access to records and stuff like that. It would definitely make sense that she was Foyle's partner in the insurance scam! I'm going over there now and talk to her. Do you know her name?"

"No, I only know her by sight. But I'll bet Mr. Packard could help you out," Ned said.

An hour later Nancy was cruising along Main Street in Mapleton, heading for the Mutual Life offices. As she stopped for a light, her eye was caught by a familiar logo on a building on the north side of the street. "Karsh's department store," she said aloud. That was the place where Michelle Ferraro worked.

On impulse, Nancy pulled over to the curb and

got out. Perhaps someone Michelle worked with —her supervisor, maybe—knew something about her relationship with Foyle, or about her salary. She walked up to the store window and peered in. It wasn't open yet, as it wasn't quite ten o'clock, but Nancy could see people inside, getting the store ready. She made a note to herself to come back later.

She was about to turn away when she suddenly found herself staring into a pair of dark, angry eyes. It was Michelle! Nancy realized with a start. She must have spotted Nancy peering in. The leopard scarf she had been wearing when Nancy questioned her the day before was draped around her neck. She was twirling the ends with her fingers and glaring venomously at Nancy. After a second Michelle tossed her head and sauntered away.

Nancy headed back to her car, a little shaken by the fierce expression she had seen on the girl's face. Getting in, she drove the two blocks to the Mutual Life offices, where she found a space at the very back of the parking lot behind the annex, in the shade of some trees.

Nancy went into the annex and headed for Joe Packard's second-floor office. Andy Feinberg, Ned's office mate, was just going into their office with another guy as she arrived. He gave her a friendly look and a wave, and Nancy smiled back.

Packard was glad to see her, but when she told him why she was there, his smile faded. "Do you really think that Foyle's murder has something to do with insurance fraud?" he asked, sounding anxious.

"It's a possibility," Nancy replied, sitting in a chair near his desk.

"What about Michelle Ferraro?" asked Packard.

"She's still on the list of suspects. I saw her this morning at Karsh's, and she gave me a really nasty look," Nancy told him. "But a glare isn't proof of anything. I still have to check out the fraud idea."

He nodded. "Yes, I suppose you do," he agreed. "I hate to think that any of our employees could be stealing from the company, but I guess it's possible. Now, let's see." He pulled out a directory of telephone extensions and studied it.

"The girl works in accounting, eh?" he murmured. "Well, it's not any of these women, because none of them is young and blond. And the others are men. So it must be this name right here." He pointed to a spot on the directory. "Libby Cartwright."

Nancy thanked him and went up a flight to the accounting department on the third floor. A man at the photocopy machine pointed out Libby Cartwright's cubicle, and Nancy went over.

"Miss Cartwright?" she said.

The girl in the cubicle turned around and Nancy had to work hard to keep a straight face. It *was* the girl from Conchita's. But Libby certainly looked different this morning. Her blond hair, now mousse-free, was pulled back into a bun, and she had on no makeup. She wore glasses, a demure high-necked blouse, and a gray suit.

"Yes?" Libby replied, and Nancy recognized her high, slightly breathless voice at once.

"My name's Nancy Drew. I'm a private investigator," Nancy told her. "I'd like to talk to you about Toby Foyle."

Libby's blue eyes immediately filled with tears. "Oh, poor Toby," she said sadly. "It's so tragic, isn't it? We were just getting to know each other when it happened."

"Uh—how long had you known Mr. Foyle?" Nancy asked.

"I had only two dates with him," Libby told her. She pulled out a tissue and dabbed at her eyes. "But it seemed as if we had known each other forever. I mean, we felt like old friends from the moment we met. I think he had that effect on people. You must know what I mean—you worked with him."

"Worked with him?" Nancy repeated blankly. "What makes you think that?"

"You mean you didn't work with him?" Libby looked surprised. "Oh, excuse me, I assumed—Well, he was a private eye, too, you know."

"I—I see," Nancy said. This young woman seemed a bit flaky. Could she really believe that Foyle was a detective? "Did he tell you that?"

"Sure," Libby replied. "That's how we met, actually. I was at a club last weekend, and I was talking to my friend about how I've always had a crush on Jim Brandon—you know, the private eye in the TV show 'Brandon.' Anyway, Toby overheard and told me he was a private eye, too." She gave a forlorn little smile. "I guess the rest is history."

"I guess it is," Nancy agreed. Suddenly she felt sorry for Libby. Though she was older than Nancy, there was something innocent, almost childlike, about her. Nancy didn't think she was capable of lying. Obviously Libby had been blind to the real Toby Foyle.

Still, Nancy thought, she might as well mention the settlement Foyle had received and see if it had any effect on Libby.

"Did you know that Mr. Foyle recently received a hundred thousand dollars from Mutual Life, as a claim settlement for a car accident?" Nancy asked.

Libby's eyes went round with astonishment. "That was *Toby?*" she said breathlessly. "I heard about that claim. Everyone was talking about it, because it's the third settlement in the last six months, and Mutual Life almost never settles. But I had no idea it was Toby who got it!"

Just then Libby's phone buzzed, and she picked it up. "Yes, Ms. Johnson," she said into the mouthpiece after a moment. "Which records do you need?"

Nancy glanced at her watch. This was getting her nowhere. She'd be better off trying to check out Michelle's salary at Karsh's. She waved goodbye to Libby, who waved back distractedly.

After she left the annex, Nancy went down the block to a pay phone and called Ned. She told him about her interview with Libby, then hung up and headed for her car.

She was about ten feet away when she noticed that the small triangular window on the driver's side of the Mustang had been smashed. Broken glass littered the asphalt around the blue car. Alarmed, Nancy rushed over and opened the door. Her eyes widened at the sight that greeted her.

The cloth upholstery of the driver's seat was in tatters. Someone had obviously slashed it to bits with a knife or a razor blade. A piece of paper was taped to the back of the seat.

Her heart pounding, Nancy pulled it off and turned it over. On the other side was a single, neatly typed sentence: "Next time it'll be your face, Nancy Drew."

Chapter Ten

NANCY CAUGHT her breath. The message was clear, and she had a feeling she knew who had sent it. The vicious knife slashes immediately brought one person to mind—Michelle Ferraro.

Michelle had the opportunity, too, Nancy realized. She worked only two blocks away, and she knew Nancy was in the neighborhood. She could have watched where Nancy went, waited until she left her car, and then vandalized it.

Well, if Michelle thinks I'll back off after this, she's got another think coming! Nancy thought, fuming. No way would she drop her investigation. Not when Ned's future was at stake!

Nancy debated for a moment, but finally decided against calling the police. It was already noon, and she had a lot to do that day. Answering their questions would only slow her down. Besides, she didn't want to have to tell them *why* she was being threatened. She had a feeling Detective Matsuo wouldn't take kindly to a teenage private investigator trying to upset his open-and-shut case against Ned.

Reaching inside her purse, Nancy fished around for her spiral notepad. Gingerly, she folded the threatening note and slid it between the sheets in the pad. Later, when she got home, she'd test it for prints.

Nancy leaned against the Mustang and crossed her arms over her chest. I suppose I'd better check my other suspects out, too, she thought. It's possible that Libby Cartwright was putting on that little-girl act to throw me off the trail. Then she could have slipped out here and done this while I was phoning Ned.

With a last look at the vandalized car, Nancy turned and went back to the Mutual Life offices. The flashing light in the lobby indicated that an elevator was coming. Nancy stood to one side as the doors opened and a crowd of people got off. Suddenly she found herself face-to-face with Wally Biggs. The plump man's eyes bulged at the sight of her.

"You have a lot of nerve hanging around here," he snapped at her. Then, his cheeks flushed with satisfaction, he turned on his heel.

"Her boyfriend is the one who killed that fellow in the warehouse the other day," Nancy heard him saying to his companion. "I always knew that Nickerson character was no good."

Her heart heavy, Nancy got into the elevator and pushed the button for the third floor. So far, the day was turning out to be a nightmare!

Nancy got out on the third floor and was walking toward Libby's cubicle when she almost bumped into Libby. She had just come out of an office whose nameplate read "Vera Johnson."

"Hey, I thought you left," Libby said, falling into step beside Nancy.

"I, uh, think I dropped my favorite pen near your desk," Nancy improvised.

"Oh. Sorry I didn't get to say goodbye—Ms. Johnson needed some records, and when Ms. Johnson needs something, she always needs it right away." Libby grimaced.

"Have you been in Ms. Johnson's office all this time?" Nancy asked casually.

"Sure have," Libby said with a sigh.

Looking at the blond girl, Nancy thought again that she was just too innocent to lie. And she had an alibi. So that left only Michelle Ferraro!

"You know, I still can't believe Toby got so much money out of Mutual Life," Libby said, breaking into Nancy's thoughts as they reached her cubicle. "It's not easy. Why, I had to go to the hospital for appendicitis a few months ago, after I'd been working here for two months and twenty-one days. Know what? They wouldn't pay my bill. Said I hadn't been with the company long enough. My benefits didn't take effect until three months after my hiring date."

"That's terrible," Nancy said sympathetically.

She bent down and pretended to look around for her pen.

"And then I heard this other story," Libby rattled on, "about this poor guy who'd worked here all his life. His wife was in the hospital with a long illness, and just because he'd forgotten to file some paperwork, the guy was stuck with all of her hospital expenses after she died. It wiped him out completely!"

"Unbelievable," Nancy commented distractedly. She straightened up. "Well, my pen isn't here. I guess I must have lost it somewhere else."

"Gee, that's too bad," said Libby, shaking her head.

"Anyway," Nancy said, "I've got to go now."

Libby smiled. "Have a nice day."

Nancy left the building, got into her vandalized car, and headed up the street to Karsh's. She was tired of wasting time. If she was going to prove that Michelle had killed Foyle, she had to get proof now!

At the store Nancy asked a salesgirl where she could find Michelle Ferraro. She was told that Michelle worked in the accessories department on the ground floor.

Nancy headed over there. She approached a prim-looking woman who was arranging belts on a rack. "Excuse me, I'm looking for Michelle Ferraro."

The woman gave Nancy an icy stare. "Miss Ferraro is not available," she said haughtily.

"Oh, that's too bad." Nancy swallowed her

frustration. Nothing was going right! She managed to give the woman a pleasant smile as she asked, "Do you know when she's coming back?"

"I couldn't say," the woman replied.

Nancy stared at the woman, confused. Why was this saleslady treating her like a criminal? "Well, then, could you tell me when she left?" she asked. At least she might be able to establish whether Michelle had had time to vandalize her car.

The woman sniffed disapprovingly. "Miss Ferraro has been gone for at least an hour," she informed Nancy. Then she turned firmly back to her work.

An hour? thought Nancy. So it could have been Michelle! she was thinking excitedly. The time fits, the method fits—she had to be the one who slashed my seat. Now, if I can prove it, I might be getting somewhere!

By evening, though, Nancy was discouraged. At home she'd used dusting powder to check the threatening note for fingerprints, but there were none. There were also none, other than her own, on the slashed seat.

She doubted that trying to trace the paper or the typewriter would help, either. The paper was generic looking, and the typeface had no revealing breaks or imperfections that would link it to a particular machine. How was she going to prove Michelle was involved? Michelle had covered her tracks perfectly!

Just then the phone rang.

"Hi, Nancy," George said when Nancy answered. "I tracked down a list of the companies that rent space in that warehouse."

"Terrific. How'd you do it?" Nancy asked.

"I called up the realtors for the building and told them I was with the FBI and that we suspected someone was hiding contraband in that warehouse," George replied. Nancy heard her giggle over the line. "It was pretty funny. They practically fell over themselves to get me the list."

"I believe it. I'll bet they're pretty shaken up since the murder," said Nancy. "They probably think the warehouse is jinxed."

"It's a pretty long list," George went on. "About half the businesses in Mapleton are on it, I'd say. And there's one name you're not going to like—Mutual Life. They've been keeping old records there for years."

Nancy's heart sank. That meant that Ned could have had the key to the warehouse. This was another nail in his coffin! "You're right. The prosecution could use that against Ned in court," she said glumly. "But tell me something. Is Karsh's department store on the list?"

"Let's see—Karsh's, Karsh's—yes, it's here," George replied after a minute. "Why?"

"That's where Michelle works," Nancy told her. "It's one more link between her and the murder. Now if only I could get some hard evidence!"

After she and George talked about the case for a few more minutes, Nancy hung up. She had promised to help Hannah with dinner that night, so she went down to the kitchen.

"Oh, Nancy, I forgot to tell you earlier," Hannah said as she handed Nancy a head of lettuce. "Brenda Carlton called twice today. She said something about your owing her a scoop. She was very—er—persistent."

Nancy smiled. Hannah really meant that Brenda was being a pain in the neck, as usual.

"Thanks," she said, taking the lettuce and beginning to tear it up for salad. "If she calls again, tell her I'm working on a story that will knock her socks off." I just hope that's true, she added to herself.

Over dinner Nancy told her father about what had happened at Mutual Life earlier and about having seen Michelle Ferraro. He was very concerned when he heard about her slashed car seat.

"Nancy, I really think we ought to tell the police about it," he said worriedly. "I don't like the idea of that young woman threatening you. What if she decides to act on her threat?"

"Dad, even if I told the police, they don't have any evidence to arrest Michelle," Nancy pointed out. "And it would scare her. I don't want to make her any more nervous than she is—until I find hard proof that ties her to the murder."

Her father frowned, but finally he said, "All right, but be careful."

When dinner was over, Nancy went out to her car, patched the broken window with a piece of plastic, and covered the torn seat with a sheepskin throw. With the case taking up all her time, she didn't know when she'd be able to have it professionally fixed. Then she drove out to Mapleton to see Ned. She knew he must be going half crazy, cooped up in his house.

Mrs. Nickerson answered the door. "Hello, Nancy," she said with an anxious smile. "Any news yet?"

"I'm working on it," Nancy told her. She didn't want to raise Mrs. Nickerson's hopes falsely, but she didn't want to discourage her, either. "I think I'm onto something—I'm just looking for proof to support my theory."

"Hey, Nan," Ned called from the den. "I'm cuing up a movie on the VCR. You're just in time."

With a smile at Mrs. Nickerson, Nancy went in and joined him.

They watched *The Heart's Reckoning.* It was one of Nancy's favorite romantic movies, but she found herself unable to concentrate on it. Her mind was too busy going over the angles of the case. She needed proof, hard evidence. But *where* was she going to get it?

"Hey," Ned said as the credits started to roll. "You didn't pay any more attention to that movie than I did. What's on your mind?"

Nancy sighed. "Just the case, I guess."

"Mmm. It's funny," Ned said with a crooked smile. "I used to get ticked off sometimes when you were working on a case because you were so single-minded about it. But now that it's *my* neck in the noose, I'm glad that you're so diligent."

Nancy twisted on the couch and put her arms

around him. "I love your neck, Ned, and I want to protect it," she said with a smile.

Ned smiled, but then his expression grew serious. "You know," he said after a moment, "I've been thinking about some things these past couple of days."

"Like what?" Nancy asked softly.

"Oh, like how this whole mess got started," Ned said. "It never would have happened if I hadn't been so set on proving myself."

Nancy frowned. "At work, you mean?"

"At work," Ned agreed, shrugging. Then he looked into her eyes. "But also, I think I was trying to prove something to you. I was trying to show you that I could be like you."

"Oh, Ned," Nancy said. She was amazed that they could have misunderstood each other. "I'm the one who should say I'm sorry. I wasn't very supportive of you." She kissed him lightly on the nose. "Listen, the last thing in the world that I want is for you to be like me! Don't ever, ever think you have to prove anything to me. You're smart, you're fantastic looking, and you're incredibly sweet. I already know you're the most wonderful guy in the world."

Ned's brown eyes were full of love as he leaned in for a kiss. Their lips met, and Nancy savored the sweet, giddy feeling that always swept over her when they touched.

Finally they drew apart. Nancy sat back on the couch. "Wow!" she murmured. Then she caught sight of the VCR's clock. "Hey, I'd better get going. Dad'll worry if I'm not home by midnight."

"I'll walk you out to the car," Ned offered. Grinning, he added, "It's dark out there. Wouldn't want the bogeyman to get you."

At the car Ned took Nancy into his arms again. "I love you, Nancy," he said tenderly.

"I love you, too," she whispered. Nancy reached down and unlocked the car door, then turned back for another kiss.

Out of the corner of her eye she saw a tiny flame flare in the darkness about ten yards away. Before she could see what it was, there was a soft *whoosh*.

Then, in an instant, the Mustang was engulfed in white-hot flames!

Chapter Eleven

A FLAME LICKED OUT and caught the sleeve of Nancy's blouse before she could react. Her scream was cut off as a strong arm grabbed her around the waist.

"Roll away from it!" Ned shouted, pulling Nancy out into the street.

Ned and Nancy hit the ground together, then rolled over and over, away from the blazing car. Through the roaring flames, Nancy thought she heard an engine start up in the distance.

"Hey, I don't think the gas tank is going to blow," Ned said in her ear after a moment. "Look, the fire's dying down some already."

Nancy sat up and stared at the fireball, breathing hard. The flames were orange now, shot with blue. As she watched, they began to shrink until they were just licking at the bottom of the car.

"Ned, are you okay?" she asked anxiously.

"I'm fine," came his reply. "What about you? Did you get burned at all?"

Nancy looked down at her arm. "My shirt is scorched, that's all. The flame must have gone out when I rolled over on the ground. Ned, if it hadn't been for you, I might not have gotten away so easily." Suddenly her teeth began to chatter as she realized what a close call they'd just had.

"Shhh. It's okay. We're both fine," Ned said, stroking her hair.

"Ned! Nancy!" Ned's mother's frantic voice came from the Nickersons' porch. "What happened? Are you two all right?"

Ned jumped to his feet. "Over here, Mom. We're fine," he called. "But you'd better call the fire department."

"Your father's already done that." Mrs. Nickerson rushed over to Nancy and Ned. "What happened?" she asked in a quavering voice.

Ned and Nancy exchanged a glance. "I guess there was a gas leak somewhere, and I made a spark when I scraped my keys against the car," Nancy said quickly. She didn't want to alarm Ned's mother.

"Oh, goodness. Look at you, Nancy—your blouse is singed. Oh, I'm so glad you weren't hurt! Come inside, you two."

As they walked toward the house, Ned took

Nancy's arm and said in a low voice, "There wasn't any accident with the keys. You saw something, didn't you? What was it?"

In a whisper, Nancy told him about the glowing flame she had seen just before the fire broke out. "I have a feeling someone laid a trail of gasoline right to my car, and then lit it from down the street," she said. Nancy sniffed. Now that she thought about it, she had noticed the faint odor of gasoline in the warm night air. "We're just lucky the car didn't blow up. Hey, where are you going?"

Ned was jogging toward the Mustang, where now only a few small flames flickered on the ground. "I want to check something out," he said over his shoulder. "Mom, we'll be right in."

When they got near the car, Nancy saw with relief that it was barely damaged. The fire had died so quickly that there were only a few blisters and scorch marks on the blue paint.

"Wow, I can't believe this!" she said.

"I can," Ned replied. He was gazing at the path the fire had made. Flames sputtered along a line that stretched into the shadows down the block. Nancy watched as Ned wrapped the tail of his shirt around his hand and opened the flap that covered the gas tank cap.

"What are you looking for?" she asked him, leaning over his shoulder.

"Let me show you something. See those marks?" Ned pointed at some faint, bright scratch marks around the keyhole of the gas cap.

"Someone tried to get to the tank!" Nancy exclaimed, horrified.

He nodded. "You're lucky you have one of these locking caps instead of the screw-in kind," he said. "Otherwise this scene would have been a whole lot worse. If the fire had actually made it to the gas tank, your car would have been destroyed —and we might not be standing here right now."

Nancy shivered. "Someone wants me off this case pretty badly," she murmured.

"I'll tell you something," Ned went on. "It's my guess that whoever did this doesn't know too much about cars and probably got the idea from watching the bad guys' limos explode on TV. But in real life it takes more than just a flash fire under the body to ignite the gas in the tank. You need intense, sustained heat. And even then, the gas doesn't always explode. It just burns."

"Ned," Nancy said slowly, "I'll bet Michelle Ferraro doesn't know a whole lot about cars."

"Maybe," he said worriedly. "Nancy, this case is getting dangerous. I don't want you to get killed for my sake. Maybe it *is* time to back off."

"No way," Nancy told him firmly. "I'm not giving up. No one is going to kill me, and no one is going to talk me out of solving this mystery, Ned. It's just too important."

Just then Nancy heard the wail of an approaching fire engine. Seconds later a hook-and-ladder truck careened around the corner, its roof lights twirling, and came to a halt in front of the Nickersons' house. A police car pulled up behind it. Up and down the block, Nancy saw rectangles of light as the Nickersons' neighbors began opening their doors and peering out.

"Hey, kids, where's the fire?" a burly firefighter in a canvas coat called to Nancy and Ned.

"It *was* under this car," Ned called back. "But it's died down already."

The man clumped over in his hip boots and gazed at the Mustang. "Hey, Lewis—get the hose over here!" he called. Two more firefighters trotted over with a hose, and the burly man directed a stream of water at the flames that were still flickering here and there under the body of the car. Then he asked Nancy and Ned, "Any idea how it happened?"

Nancy told him about seeing the light down the street. "I'd say it was thirty or forty feet in back of the car," she finished. "There was this noise, and then *poof!* the car went up."

"Uh-huh," the fireman said. He squinted down the street where Nancy had pointed. "Not much light out here," he remarked. "Did you see anyone?"

"Hey, Wilson!" called another one of the firefighters. "I've got the chief on the line. Do we need any backup?"

"Nah," the guy with Nancy and Ned replied. "Tell him it's under control." He turned back to Nancy and repeated his question.

Nancy frowned, trying to remember. "No, I didn't see anyone," she replied. "But I did *hear* something. Right after the explosion, I heard a car start. And then someone drove away."

"Uh-huh," said Wilson. Pulling a flashlight out of a loop on his long coat, he began to walk slowly down the street, peering at the ground. Nancy and Ned followed.

After he had gone about thirty feet, Wilson knelt down on one knee and played his light on the asphalt. Then he bent over. A moment later he stood, holding something between his thumb and forefinger.

"What is it?" Nancy asked, her excitement mounting.

Wilson held out his hand. In his palm lay a charred strip of cardboard. "It's the remains of a match," he told her.

"I think I found something," Ned said suddenly from farther down the street. He was pointing at a blackened mound, barely visible against the asphalt.

Wilson strode over and poked at the mound. Then he picked it up and sniffed at it. "The remains of a gasoline-soaked rag," he said quietly. "Sure looks like this was arson."

After that, Wilson called over one of the police officers from the cruiser and told him about the rag. The officer glanced at Nancy and Ned, and suddenly his expression darkened.

"Hey, aren't you the guy we pulled in on that warehouse homicide?" he asked Ned sharply.

Nancy made a quick decision. "That's right, Officer," she jumped in before Ned could reply. "And we'd like to talk to Detective Matsuo right away. We have reason to believe this fire was set for reasons relating to the Foyle case."

"Nan, we don't have any hard evidence yet," Ned protested in an undertone as the officer led them to the patrol car.

"I know, but the circumstantial evidence pointing to Michelle is pretty strong," Nancy told him. "I don't think anyone is going to dispute that someone set this fire or that it was directed at me. If we can just get Matsuo to listen to us, maybe he'll do something."

Ned ran in to tell his parents where they were going, and then the two teenagers climbed into the squad car. Five minutes later they were walking up the steps of Mapleton Police Headquarters.

"I'm beginning to dislike this building," Ned said to Nancy. She squeezed his hand reassuringly.

This time they were led to Matsuo's office. The police detective was hunched behind a cluttered desk, looking tired and grumpy. "More trouble, Nickerson?" he drawled.

Ned scowled but said nothing.

Stepping forward, Nancy said, "Detective Matsuo, my name is Nancy Drew—" She got no further, though, for Matsuo interrupted her.

"I've heard of you," he said, sounding even less friendly than he had a moment ago. "You're that hotshot detective from River Heights, aren't you? An amateur." He said the word with distaste. "Didn't you tell us you were a legal secretary or something, last time you were here? It's a bad idea to lie to the police like that."

Nancy did her best to look contrite. "I'm

sorry," she said. "I had to do it. But, sir, we have something urgent to tell you. It concerns the murder of Toby Foyle."

"Oh, yeah?" said Matsuo. He leaned back and put his feet on the desk. "Well, sit down and tell me. I'm all ears."

Nancy and Ned pulled up chairs. Then, leaning forward, Nancy told him her theory about Michelle Ferraro having killed Toby Foyle in a jealous rage. She also told him about her slashed car seat and about Ned's idea that the person who had tried to torch her Mustang didn't know much about cars.

Detective Matsuo listened in silence, but Nancy noticed with a twinge of unease that he was smiling, as if he thought their story was a joke. The smile broadened as she talked on.

When Nancy had finished, Matsuo swung his feet to the floor. "It's a nice theory, Ms. Drew," he told her. His voice was almost pleasant. "It's got only one flaw."

"What's that?" Nancy asked warily.

Matsuo grinned. "I happen to be acquainted with Ms. Ferraro myself. And I know that she couldn't have slashed your car or set your suspicious fire. Want to know why?" He stood up. "Because Michelle Ferraro has been right here in our jail all day!"

Chapter Twelve

"WHAT?" Nancy and Ned said at the same time.

"Do you mean you arrested Michelle for Toby Foyle's murder?" Ned went on excitedly.

Nancy didn't think that was it, though. If Michelle hadn't staged those attacks on Nancy, then someone else had—and *that* person had to be the one they were after. She'd been on the wrong track entirely with Michelle! She put a hand on Ned's arm, shaking her head.

"Nice try, Nickerson," Matsuo said. "But your friend already knows that theory's no good. No, it seems Ms. Ferraro has been stealing. The cameras in the department store finally caught her at it, and her boss called us this morning. We picked her up at work at ten-thirty, and since she couldn't post bail, she's been here all day."

Nancy nodded slowly. "So *that's* where Michelle got the money to pay for all that stereo equipment," she murmured, half to herself.

"Very observant of you," Matsuo said. Then he suppressed a yawn. "Okay, we'll look into these attacks, Ms. Drew. But I'm sure you've made some enemies with all your past cases. You've sent a few criminals to jail in your time. Any one of them might be out to get you. I have to tell you, the fact that you ruined the evidence from the first car incident by not calling us in to look at it doesn't make our job any easier. We'll have to start from scratch and conduct this investigation in a logical way."

"But isn't it *logical* to think the attacks on my car might have something to do with the case I'm working on right now?" Nancy asked evenly.

"We'll look into it," Matsuo repeated. "And I would appreciate it if you'd keep out of it from now on and let the police do their job. Now ask Merriwell out there to give you a ride home. It's almost one-thirty in the morning. I, for one, am beat."

Nancy and Ned got up and left the office. Outside, Ned turned to her. "I told you we shouldn't have gone to the police," he said, sounding frustrated. "All it did was get Matsuo on your back as well as mine."

"I'm sorry, Ned." Nancy felt awful. He was right, she knew. In her eagerness to pin the crime on Michelle, she had jumped the gun.

And who knows what clues I might have missed while I was chasing after evidence to fit my theory about Michelle? Nancy wondered miserably. Thanks to my mistake, the real criminal has had all this time to cover his tracks. How will I ever solve this case?

She and Ned rode back to his house in silence. When they got there, Ned's parents greeted them anxiously. Nancy listened while Ned gave them an edited account of what had happened at the police station. She noticed that he didn't tell them that their prime suspect had just been cleared. Nancy guessed he didn't want to upset them further.

"Nancy, your father called," Mrs. Nickerson told her when Ned had finished. "He's waiting up until you get home. Can we drive you?"

"Thanks for the offer, but if my car still runs I won't need to bother you," Nancy told her.

Ned walked her out to her car and stood by while she started the engine. In spite of what it had been through, the Mustang seemed to be working all right. "I'll call you in the morning," she told Ned. "And, Ned—I really am sorry. I guess I blew it tonight, huh?"

Ned gave her a weak smile. "Hey, it's just a little setback, that's all," he said. "We'll start again tomorrow."

Tomorrow, Nancy thought as she headed home. Tomorrow is Tuesday. Two days until the grand jury!

* * *

"What's your next move?" asked Carson Drew the following morning as he and Nancy were having breakfast.

Nancy swallowed a bite of toast. "I'm going to backtrack," she said. She'd lain awake a good part of the night, going over the case in her mind. "I was too quick to drop the idea that Foyle was killed to prevent him from spilling the beans about the insurance scam. Michelle just seemed like such a perfect villain that I didn't bother to do the things I should have."

"Like what?" her father wanted to know.

"Like check Dr. Meyers's alibi for the time of the murder," Nancy replied. "Like find out how much money is in Foyle's bank account."

Her father nodded approvingly. "Smart. If there's a lot less than a hundred thousand dollars in there, that's a clear sign that he split the payment with someone else." He took a sip of coffee, then said, "But details about other people's accounts aren't freely given out. How will you get around that?"

"Chief McGinnis can call the Mapleton police and find out for me—if I can talk him into it," Nancy answered, grinning. "He said he owed me a favor, after all the times I've helped the River Heights police."

Nancy's father grinned back at her. "Good luck," he said. "And please let me know if there's anything I can do to help."

After her father went to work, Nancy called the River Heights police chief and told him what she needed. As she guessed, he did resist for a while, but finally agreed to call his colleagues in Mapleton and find out what he could.

Twenty minutes later he called Nancy back. "I had to wait for a while, but finally I managed to slip the question in," he said. "It seems Toby Foyle had a grand total of twenty-five thousand two hundred and seven dollars and change in his account. Nowhere near a hundred grand."

"All right!" Nancy was elated by the news. At last, she thought, I'm on the right track!

"Thanks, Chief," she said fervently. "Now I owe *you* one!"

The chief groaned. "Do me a favor," he said. "Just stay out of trouble for a while."

"I'll do my best," Nancy told him, laughing. She hung up and immediately dialed Bess's number.

"Bess, I need you to use your acting talents again," she said when Bess came on the line. "And George's as well. Can you call her and have her come to your house at eleven? I'll pick you both up."

"Sure thing," Bess agreed. "Hey, do you think I've got a future in Hollywood?"

"Absolutely," Nancy said, chuckling.

After she hung up, she called Information and got the address of Dr. Meyers's office. Then she went upstairs to shower and dress. By a quarter to eleven she was on her way to Bess's house.

"Boy, your car looks as if it's been through a war," Bess commented as she and George climbed into the Mustang. "What happened?"

On the drive to Mapleton, Nancy filled her friends in on everything that had happened the day before, concluding with the news that Michelle Ferraro was no longer a suspect in Foyle's murder. Then she told them about the missing money from Foyle's insurance settlement, and her idea that Foyle had split the payment with someone else.

"So it looks as if the accomplice theory may be on target after all, huh?" George said.

"Right. I'm going to revive my investigation of Dr. Meyers. That's where you guys come in," Nancy said. "I need to look at his appointment book to get the names of the patients he saw the morning of Foyle's murder. And I also want to get into his office to see if I can find out where he banks."

"Let me guess," Bess said, brushing her blond hair back from her face. "You need us to create a diversion while you sneak in."

"You got it," Nancy replied with a grin.

Dr. Meyers's office was in a small brick building on Beechwood Street, right down the block from where Toby Foyle had lived. Nancy parked across the street, and the girls sat in the car until Nancy spotted Dr. Meyers leaving the building. She glanced at her watch. "Twelve-fifteen," she said. "He must be going to lunch. Let's hope he'll be out for a while."

After getting out of the car, they went into the building, checked the directory, and took the elevator up to the fourth floor, where Meyers's office was. Nancy paused outside his door.

"Okay," she said to Bess and George. "Give me a couple of seconds, then start making noise out here. Try to keep the receptionist occupied for at least five minutes."

Bess gave Nancy the thumbs-up sign. Smiling, Nancy opened the door and went inside.

The office was empty except for a pleasant-looking Asian woman who sat in a little booth at one end. "May I help you?" she asked Nancy politely.

"I'd like to make an appointment to see Dr. Meyers," Nancy began.

At that instant a bloodcurdling scream rang out from the hallway. "My hand! I think it's broken!" Bess's voice wailed. "You crushed it in the door—I'm going to sue!"

"It wasn't my fault!" Nancy heard George yell back. "You got in the way!"

The receptionist looked toward the doorway, alarmed. "Excuse me," she murmured. "I think I'd better see what the trouble is."

"Of course. I'll just wait right here," Nancy said sweetly.

The second the receptionist left the office, Nancy hurried into the booth. The doctor's appointment book was lying open on the desk, and Nancy flipped back through the pages, hunting for the previous Saturday's entries.

"Here we are," she murmured as she found the page. Meyers had had an appointment at eight-thirty the morning of Foyle's murder and another at nine-thirty, she noted. Foyle was killed about nine-fifteen.

Nancy frowned. Even supposing the first patient had left by nine, that didn't give Meyers much time to get to the warehouse and into position to kill Foyle. The warehouse was a good ten-minute drive from the center of town.

But it was still possible, she thought. She whipped out her notebook and copied down the names and telephone numbers of the two patients. She'd have to call and find out when they had arrived and left.

Nancy paused to listen. Bess and George were still arguing in the hall, and now it sounded as if the receptionist had joined in, too. Nancy smiled and headed for Dr. Meyers's private office.

The small room was dominated by a heavy mahogany desk that looked as if it had seen better days. Also, Nancy noted with a triumphant feeling, there was a door in the far wall that clearly led out to the hall. A separate entrance—Meyers could have left without his receptionist knowing!

Nancy quickly went through the drawers. In the second one she found a scrap of paper with the name T. Foyle scrawled on it. A phone number had been written down, then crossed out, and a new one written beneath it.

Nancy pocketed the scrap. It wasn't much, but it might help to prove that Meyers had had more than a professional acquaintance with Foyle. Doctors didn't usually keep their patients' phone numbers—their receptionists did.

In the fourth drawer Nancy found what she was looking for—a book of checks from

Meyers's bank. She copied the name of the bank and the account number off the top check, then replaced the book in the drawer. Just as she slid the drawer shut, the door on the far wall swung open.

Startled, Nancy looked up—and found herself staring into the furious eyes of Dr. Meyers!

Chapter Thirteen

"WHAT ARE YOU DOING in my office?" Meyers snapped indignantly.

"Uh—I was looking for a pen," Nancy improvised, hoping her alarm wasn't noticeable in her voice. "There was no one here, so I thought I'd just help myself."

"A pen?" Dr. Meyers scoffed. His pale eyes surveyed her with cold disbelief. "There are pens at the receptionist's desk. And you wouldn't have had to enter an obviously private office to get one, either. No, Ms. Drew, you were snooping. I'm beginning to think you're harassing me."

Nancy came out from behind the desk. "Are you going to call the police?" she asked evenly. Behind her back she crossed her fingers, hoping that she'd taken the right tack. If Meyers had anything to hide, he wouldn't want to call attention to himself by bringing in the authorities.

Meyers glared at her for a moment, but finally shook his head. "No, just get out of here," he growled. "And don't bother me again, or I *will* call the police."

Nancy stepped past him and out of the office. Her heart was pounding furiously, but she forced herself to keep a steady pace. She didn't want him to know how startled she'd been by his sudden appearance.

She went out into the waiting room, where the receptionist gave her a puzzled look. "Were you just in Dr. Meyers's office?" she inquired.

"Yes, I was," Nancy told her. "He doesn't think I need an appointment—all I have is a cold. So I guess I won't be bothering you. Thanks, anyway." She gave the receptionist a quick smile and ducked out of the door.

Out in the hallway she breathed a sigh of relief. Bess and George were nowhere in sight—Nancy supposed the receptionist got them to quarrel outside.

They were waiting for her at the car. "What happened?" George asked anxiously. "We were still carrying on when Dr. Meyers came back all of a sudden and went through a door down the hall. I guess he hadn't left for lunch after all. Did he catch you?"

"Red-handed," Nancy confirmed, unlocking the car door and climbing in. "But he didn't want to call the police on me. Now, don't you guys think that's interesting?"

"Why?" Bess looked briefly puzzled. Then her blue eyes lit up. "Oh, maybe that means he's got something to hide! Way to go, Nan. Did you find anything suspicious in his office?"

Nancy shrugged. "Nothing major. I did get the name of his bank and his checking account number, though," she said. "I'm hoping my dad will be able to pull some strings and find out if he's made any large deposits lately. Come on. Let's go to Ned's house. I need to make some calls."

When they got there, Ned answered the door. His parents were out, and he was alone in the house. He seemed overjoyed to see them. Poor Ned, Nancy thought, he really hasn't been able to leave the house for the past three days!

After they'd settled in the living room, Nancy told him about the new angle she was investigating, and about her adventure at Dr. Meyers's office.

"So this case really *does* have something to do with the insurance scam after all," Ned said excitedly. "That makes me feel like less of an idiot."

"It *might,* Ned," Nancy said cautiously. "We still don't have any proof, and I don't want to jump to conclusions again."

Bess was sitting on the carpet. "Hey, do you think Meyers and Foyle planned the scam *before* Foyle's accident?" she asked. "What if it turned out they rigged the whole thing, including the accident?"

"That could be," Nancy responded. "Or he

might have had a real accident and then decided to take advantage of the situation to get the insurance money. But I *am* beginning to think Foyle wasn't the main brain behind this fraud. He kept only a quarter of the money, don't forget. Maybe he was just a pawn." She sighed. "But before I start jumping the gun again, let's see what my dad can find out for us."

Going to the Nickersons' kitchen, she picked up the phone and dialed Carson Drew's office number. "Dad," she began after they said hello, "your friend Bill Graham is a bigwig with"—she consulted the name she had written down—"Second National Bank of Illinois, isn't he?"

"Yes, why?" Carson Drew wanted to know. "Do I sense that you're about to ask me to do something that's not quite kosher?"

Nancy laughed. "You know me too well," she confessed. "Listen, can you get some information about an account for me? All I need to know is if the person who has the account recently made any large deposits. To the tune of seventy-five thousand dollars or so."

Carson whistled. "Sounds like you're onto something," he said. "I'll see what I can do, and I'll call you as soon as I know anything."

"Thanks, Dad." Nancy gave him the account number. "I'll be waiting to hear from you."

Next Nancy called the woman who had the eight-thirty appointment with Dr. Meyers on the day Foyle was killed. From her voice, Nancy guessed the woman was elderly. She pondered for a while, then said she wasn't sure when she had left Dr. Meyers's office, but she didn't think she could have been there more than half an hour.

Nancy thanked her and hung up. Then she tried calling the woman who had the nine-thirty appointment, but there was no answer.

So, Nancy thought, hanging up again, Dr. Meyers was alone for at least some time between nine and nine-thirty that morning. During that time he could have raced over to the warehouse, met Foyle, and killed him.

A little later Nancy's father called to report that his friend at the bank was in a meeting until later that afternoon. Nancy swallowed her impatience and settled in to wait. Bess and George went out to buy sandwiches and sodas, and the three girls ate with Ned and talked about the case.

At three-thirty the Nickersons' phone rang again. Ned answered and passed the receiver to Nancy. "It's your dad," he said excitedly.

"Dad," Nancy said into the phone. "Any news?"

"I'm not sure." Carson Drew's voice sounded puzzled. "Bill Graham tells me Meyers made several cash deposits to his account in the last two weeks. The total amount of the deposits is a little under twenty-five thousand dollars."

Nancy saw why her father was confused. "So where's the other fifty thousand?" she asked. "The settlement Foyle got was for a hundred thousand dollars, but he kept only a quarter of it. Did Meyers put the rest in another account?"

"Not in Second National Bank," Carson told

her. "Bill said Meyers has no other accounts there."

Nancy thought for a moment. "Well, maybe he put it in another bank. It would be foolish of him to keep it all in one place," she said. "But we've finally got a real link between Meyers, Foyle, and the insurance scam! Dad, this is great! Thanks a million."

Nancy hung up and told her friends the news. Ned's face lit up. "We're getting close, Nancy," he said. "I can feel it."

Suddenly George spoke up. "I don't mean to rain on anyone's parade," she said hesitantly, looking across the kitchen table at Nancy, "but there is one thing about the case that's bothering me."

"What's that?" Nancy asked.

"It seems so small-scale," George began.

Bess cut in with a little shriek. "You call a hundred thousand dollars 'small scale'?" she demanded.

"No, wait a second." Nancy was struck by George's point. "I see what you mean, George. Insurance claims can be much higher—in the millions sometimes. A hundred thousand is *not* that much money, especially when you're splitting it."

"Right," George said, nodding. "I mean, it doesn't seem like enough to plan a major fraud over. They were risking a lot, and you'd think the reward would be bigger, since the stakes were so high."

A frown creased Nancy's forehead. "Toby

Foyle found out just how high they were," she said, speaking half to herself.

Ned had been looking back and forth at the two girls as they spoke. "What are you getting at?" he wanted to know.

"I'm not sure," Nancy answered slowly. "But I think George may have an important point. One that could help us crack this case." She snapped her fingers as she remembered something. "I should have thought of this earlier. Libby Cartwright told me that Foyle's was the third settlement Mutual Life had paid out in the last six months. She mentioned how unusual that was."

"So?" Ned prompted.

"So maybe this scam is bigger than we've been thinking," Nancy said. "Maybe Meyers filed a few of these hard-to-verify false claims, with the cooperation of 'victims' who wanted some easy money. It would make sense." She looked at Ned. "Also, it would help explain why Meyers had to kill Foyle. Foyle got scared when you started looking into his claim. Maybe he even told Meyers he wouldn't take the fall alone—and that made Foyle too big a risk. If he spilled the beans, then Meyers would lose a lot more than just a few thousand dollars. He's in deep."

Ned tapped his fingers on the kitchen table. "How can we find out for sure?"

"Call Mr. Packard," Nancy said. "Ask him to check out any claims signed by Meyers in the past six or seven months. If he finds any that were settled for moderate amounts of money—amounts that the company might be willing to settle—get the names of the claimants, and I'll see what I can find out from them."

"Okay," Ned agreed. He picked up the phone and dialed his work number. After a brief conversation with the receptionist, he put his hand over the mouthpiece.

"Packard is at the Chicago office today," he whispered. "What should I do?"

"Ask for Andy Feinberg," Nancy whispered back. "He's your friend—he'll help you out."

Bess gave Nancy a worried glance. Nancy knew what she was thinking. What if Andy had the same reaction as some of Ned's other "friends," like that guy in the restaurant or Wally Biggs?

He won't, Nancy told herself. He was nice to me yesterday in the office. He'll help—won't he?

"Hi, Andy," Ned said after a minute, and Nancy could hear the nervousness in his voice. "It's Ned Nickerson. . . . What's that? . . . No, I'm all right." As he listened, a smile spread across his face. "Hey, thanks for saying that, Andy. I appreciate it.

"Listen, could I ask a favor?" Ned asked at last. "I need you to look up some old claims for me. . . ."

Fifteen minutes later Ned hung up. He was grinning broadly. "Andy's on my side," he said.

Nancy hugged him. "Oh, Ned, that's just great!" she said sincerely.

"Did you get anything from him?" George asked.

"Sure did." Ned held up a piece of paper he'd used to take notes on. "Here are names and phone numbers from two more of Meyers's claims. Both were settled—one for eighty thousand dollars and one for ninety-two thousand. Andy investigated one of them, and Wally Biggs did the other."

Nancy had already picked up the phone and was dialing the first number.

When a woman's voice answered, Nancy asked, "May I speak to"—she checked Ned's paper—"Marian Davis?"

"This is Marian Davis," the woman replied. "Who's calling?"

Nancy looked at Ned and made a thumbs-up sign. "Ms. Davis, my name is Nancy Drew," she said. "I'm a private investigator, and I'm looking into an insurance claim you filed on February fourth with Mutual Life."

There was a gasp on the other end of the line and then a click. The woman had hung up.

Nancy put the phone down and turned to her friends. "Guys," she said, "I think we just hit the jackpot!"

Chapter Fourteen

"HOORAY!" BESS CRIED. "That was the quickest confession I ever heard of. What did she say?"

"Well, she didn't actually confess," Nancy had to admit. "But she did gasp and hang up on me the minute I mentioned Mutual Life. I'm sure she's part of the fraud. And if we take this evidence to Detective Matsuo, he'll *have* to listen to us. He can't ignore a suspect with as strong a motive as Dr. Meyers."

Ned's face lit up. "Nancy, you're brilliant!" He grabbed her and twirled her around the kitchen. When she finally collapsed, laughing, into a chair, he grabbed George and twirled *her* around. "You're brilliant, too!" he cried.

"Hey, I feel left out," Bess joked.

"Well, you shouldn't," Nancy told her. "If it

wasn't for your terrific acting ability, we'd never have gotten this far."

Grinning, Bess tossed her long blond hair and said, "You'll have to speak to my agent about my fees."

"Now I *really* feel like celebrating," Ned said. Then his face fell. "But after what happened at Mama's the other day, I don't feel like going out in public just yet."

"I have an idea," said Nancy. "Why don't you all come to my house? We could make a big dinner, and it would give Ned a chance to get out of the house. Let me call Hannah and see if it's all right with her."

The Drews' housekeeper was pleased with the idea. "Especially if *you're* cooking, Nancy," she teased. "Yes, I think a party would be grand. I'll bake a cake."

"Thanks! See you soon," Nancy said, and hung up. "Let's hit the road," she called to her friends. "We've got some serious cooking to do!"

"Mmm. Mexican, French, and Chinese food," Carson Drew said thoughtfully. "And a German chocolate cake for dessert." His eyes twinkled. "A strange combination, but I must say it was delicious. My compliments to the chefs!"

It was later that evening, and Nancy, Ned, Bess, and George were sitting around the Drews' dining room table with Nancy's father and Hannah. They had just finished a monster meal—Nancy and Ned had made tacos, Bess had supplied an enormous salade niçoise, and George had put together her specialty, cold Chinese noodles with sesame sauce. As promised, Hannah had baked a rich chocolate cake to finish off the meal.

Bess pushed her chair back from the table and groaned. "I know I just gained back those five pounds it took me so long to lose," she said ruefully. "But it was worth it."

"Work it off. Why don't you play tennis with me?" George suggested.

A look of shock crossed Bess's face. "Tennis? Ugh—too strenuous!"

George grinned at Nancy. "I need a partner. Every time Nancy and I have a tennis date, she calls me at the last minute and says she's got a new case and can't make it."

Nancy returned the smile absently. During dinner, her thoughts had strayed back to the case. Though she didn't want to say anything to spoil the festive mood, she was worried.

Just before sitting down to eat, her father had taken her aside. "You've done a terrific job," he'd told her. "You've found a suspect with a motive and, possibly, an opportunity to kill Toby Foyle. But I should tell you that we still have a lot of hard work to do. Don't forget that Ned was found at the scene, with the murder weapon in his hand. Against that, even a strong motive like the one Dr. Meyers has may not get Ned off. I think the best we can hope for at this point is reasonable doubt."

Now, thinking about what her father had said, Nancy frowned.

"Hey, what's on your mind?" Ned asked her softly.

"Huh? Oh—nothing," Nancy began. Just then the phone rang, and she got up to answer it. Her heart sank when she heard Brenda Carlton's voice on the other end of the line.

"Where's my scoop?" Brenda demanded. "I haven't heard anything from you in three days, Nancy. I know you've been avoiding me. What's wrong, can't you solve this case?"

Nancy rolled her eyes. "Brenda, I just need a little more time," she replied, forcing the annoyance out of her voice. "I'm really close, I swear."

"Close isn't good enough," Brenda snapped. "I put my story on hold for you, Nancy. Now I want something hot in return. I want a smoking gun!"

That's what I want, too! Nancy thought. Direct proof of Meyers's guilt. "I'll get it," she said aloud. "I'll call you tomorrow, okay?"

"You'd better." *Click!* Brenda had hung up.

Sighing, Nancy went back to the table.

"Who was that on the phone?" her father asked.

"Oh, just Brenda Carlton," Nancy said.

"Did you tell her you'd solved the case?" Ned asked eagerly.

"No. Um, Ned, it's not quite solved yet." Nancy winced as she saw the unhappiness in his brown eyes. "I mean, we only need a little more evidence," she hurried on. "We're almost there, but when we present the facts, I want to be sure that no one can argue with them."

"I see," Ned said heavily. "I guess we celebrated a little too soon, huh?"

"Not at all," Carson said in a hearty tone. "We've certainly got something to celebrate. With what Nancy has found out so far, I'm sure I could convince the jury that there's reasonable doubt in your case."

"Reasonable doubt?" echoed Bess. Hesitantly she asked, "Is that enough?"

"No," Nancy replied firmly. "No offense, Dad, but reasonable doubt is not good enough. There has to be no doubt at all. I *have* to clear Ned. It's the only way he can put this all behind him and get on with his life."

After that the life seemed to go out of the dinner party. A little while later Ned asked Nancy to take him home. Seeing the slump of his shoulders, Nancy felt bad, but there was nothing she could do.

They rode in silence back to Mapleton. Nancy searched for something to say that would cheer Ned up, but nothing came to her—until, at last, she was struck by an idea.

"I'm not going to come into the house with you," she told Ned as she pulled up in front of his home. "I want to stop off and ask Toby Foyle's landlady, Mrs. Godfrey, a question, and I should do it before it gets too late."

"Do you have a new lead?" Ned asked hopefully.

"Could be. I'll let you know." Secretly, Nancy crossed her fingers and hoped something would come of it. She kissed Ned goodbye, then drove over to Beechwood Street. After climbing out of her battered Mustang, she hurried up the steps and rang Mrs. Godfrey's doorbell.

"I'm sorry to bother you so late," Nancy said when Mrs. Godfrey opened the door a crack. "I just want to ask you one question."

"It's no bother," Mrs. Godfrey said. She held the door open and gestured for Nancy to come in. "I told you before that I'd like to help your young friend if I can. What's your question?"

Nancy followed Mrs. Godfrey into the living room and took a seat while the elderly woman switched off the television set.

"Mrs. Godfrey, I want you to think back to the morning Toby Foyle was killed," Nancy said once the older woman was seated in an easy chair. "Think carefully. Before he left, did he say anything to you about where he was going or whom he might be meeting?"

"No." Mrs. Godfrey frowned. "The police already asked me that question. Mr. Foyle went out and slammed the door, the way he always did. I do remember being surprised that he was up so early. Usually he didn't stir before ten."

Nancy's heart sank. It didn't look as if this line of questioning was going to get her very far. "Did anyone call or come by?" she asked.

"No one."

Nancy decided to ask one last question. It was a long shot, but worth a try. "Did you ever hear Mr. Foyle mention anyone named Meyers?" she asked without much hope.

Mrs. Godfrey rubbed the bridge of her nose

thoughtfully. "Meyers. Meyers. The name does ring a bell," she said.

"Really?" Nancy leaned forward excitedly. "How? Please try to remember, Mrs. Godfrey. This could be important."

"I'm sorry, I— Wait a moment! Now I remember." Suddenly Mrs. Godfrey sat upright in her chair. "A call came in on my telephone line. A man named Meyers called for Mr. Foyle on Friday evening, right before Mr. Foyle went out. Let's see, that would have been about a quarter to seven. Yes, that's right. I remember it because I was annoyed that Mr. Foyle was still getting calls on my line, even though he'd gotten his own phone more than a week before. But I suppose he's still listed in the book as having my number."

"Did Mr. Foyle say anything unusual during the conversation?" Nancy pressed.

Mrs. Godfrey pressed her lips into a thin line. "I'm not in the habit of listening to other people's conversations," she said disapprovingly.

If only you were! Nancy thought to herself. She was sure that Meyers had called to set up his meeting at the warehouse with Foyle. But Mrs. Godfrey's story wasn't good enough. It was another link, but it wasn't the one that would complete the chain of evidence against the doctor.

Then suddenly Nancy remembered something that made her blue eyes narrow thoughtfully. "Meyers had Foyle's new number," she muttered. "I found it in his desk drawer."

"I beg your pardon?" Mrs. Godfrey said, looking confused.

Realizing she had been talking out loud to herself, Nancy explained, "I happen to know that Meyers had Foyle's new number. So why would he call the old one?"

Mrs. Godfrey shrugged. "Maybe he didn't have the new number with him," she suggested.

"Maybe," Nancy agreed. But there was something else about the setup that bothered her. Why would Meyers give his own name if he was calling to set up a murder? Did he just assume that no one would remember the call later on? Or could it be that the call had been innocent after all?

Still pondering, Nancy thanked Mrs. Godfrey, said goodbye, and went out to her car.

She was standing by the driver's door, fumbling in her purse for her keys, when the roar of a nearby engine made her jump. Looking over her right shoulder, she was almost blinded by the headlights of an approaching car.

That car's coming awfully fast, Nancy thought. In the next instant, she realized that the car was aimed straight at her!

Chapter Fifteen

NANCY LOOKED frantically around for a place to escape, but in the narrow street, there was nowhere to go! Desperate, she threw herself onto the hood of her car. Just as she pulled her legs up, she felt a rush of air as the other car sped past.

Her heart was hammering so loud she was sure anyone who lived on the block could hear it. Nancy continued to lie facedown for a second, hugging the hood of the Mustang. Then she slid off the car and ran out into the middle of the street. If she could only get the license number or make of the car!

It was long gone, though. Nancy could barely make out its taillights several blocks away. As she watched, the tiny red lights were swallowed up by the darkness.

Taking a big, calming breath, Nancy stepped up to her car. Someone really wants me to back off, she thought. And whoever it is is scared enough to take risks to stop me. That means I must be close!

It could have been Dr. Meyers, she reasoned as she drove home. He lived only two or three blocks away. Maybe he had spotted Nancy going into Mrs. Godfrey's, rushed home for his car, driven over to Beechwood, and waited for Nancy.

Of course, it was an amazing coincidence that he just happened to see Nancy in the seconds it had taken her to get from her car to Mrs. Godfrey's door. Still, that must be what had happened.

"It's the only thing that makes sense!" Nancy exclaimed aloud. She was getting annoyed with herself. The mistake about Michelle Ferraro was making her worry so much about leaping to conclusions that she was beginning to doubt the facts!

Scowling in the darkness after getting into her car, Nancy popped a cassette into her tape player and pushed the tiny voice of doubt firmly to the back of her mind.

By Wednesday, though, Nancy's doubts had grown. She had hoped to get her slashed car seat replaced in an hour, but as it turned out, she spent nearly four hours at the auto body shop. While she waited, she thought of two more flaws in her case against Dr. Meyers.

First, there was the question of how he had slashed her car seat. How could he have known where to find her? Nancy didn't believe coincidence could have brought him to the exact spot where she was. That was stretching things too far.

The same question had to be asked about the fire at her car on Monday night. How had he found her at Ned's house?

Nancy's thoughts were interrupted by the voice of the auto repairman. "Okay, we got your seat fixed, Ms. Drew," he said. "Sure you don't want to leave the car here for a new paint job?"

She stood up and pulled out her wallet. "Thanks, but I can't spare the time right now," she said. Then, patting the Mustang's hood fondly, she added, "I'll be back in a couple of days, though, and then you can give this baby whatever it needs."

It was a warm, hazy day, and the air held the promise of rain. Nancy pushed sticky strands of reddish blond hair off her face as she drove. She stopped by Bess's house to see if her friend was home, but Bess's mother told her both Bess and George were spending the day with their grandmother.

Nancy let out a sigh of disappointment as she got back into the car. She had really been hoping to talk the case over with her friends to get it clear in her mind. Time was running out, and she still hadn't cleared Ned.

When Nancy got home, she was dismayed to see a dark-haired figure sitting on her front porch. Just what I need, she thought glumly.

"Brenda!" she called, trying to put some warmth in her voice. "I was just going to call you."

"Tell me another one," the reporter snapped. "You never did call me this morning, even though you promised you would."

"I was about to," Nancy protested weakly.

"Well, it's nearly two o'clock. I don't call this morning anymore. Look, Nancy, I'm tired of chasing you. Where's my scoop?" Brenda whined. "Am I going to have to solve this case for you?"

Fat chance! Nancy said to herself. But aloud she merely replied, "I'm almost there."

Brenda scowled. "I don't believe you," she challenged. "You're stuck. In fact, I don't think you know anything more than you knew the day Ned was arrested!"

"That's not true!" Nancy retorted.

"All right, then, prove it," Brenda flung back. "Tell me exactly what you do know. Otherwise I'll write a very unflattering piece on Ned."

Nancy closed her eyes in total frustration. Brenda was so irritating that she wanted to shake her!

"Fine," Nancy said at last. "But you'd better not print what I'm about to tell you. I can't prove it yet, and you don't want to get sued for libel, do you?"

Brenda looked smug. "Don't worry about me."

Nancy reluctantly invited Brenda in, and the

two girls went into the kitchen. Hannah was out, and Carson was at work, so the house was empty.

Nancy poured herself and Brenda tall glasses of lemonade. Then, taking a deep breath, she told Brenda about the whole case, detail by detail.

"The problem is, I can't prove Dr. Meyers actually went to the warehouse on Saturday morning," she concluded. "I can prove that he *could* have gone, but my dad says that won't be enough, with the evidence against Ned. And there are those little holes, too. I'm sure there's a way to prove the whole thing and get Meyers arrested, but I haven't found it yet."

Brenda had been writing down everything Nancy said. Now she snapped her notebook shut and said darkly, "Want to know what I think?"

Nancy didn't, really, but knew it would be rude to say so. "What?" she asked.

"I think you're completely wrong," Brenda announced. "Meyers didn't kill that guy. But you keep trying to prove he did because you can't face the truth about your boyfriend, Nancy. You can't admit that Ned is guilty."

"Brenda!" Nancy was furious.

"It's obvious there's another side to Ned," Brenda went on. She waved her hands dramatically. "A dark, criminal side. He, Foyle, and Dr. Meyers were in league to steal money from the insurance company. But something went wrong." She leaned forward over the kitchen table, lowering her voice. "*Very* wrong. They had a falling-out. Foyle was going to talk, and so Ned killed him."

Nancy turned away, disgusted. How could Brenda spout that kind of nonsense? The very idea of Ned having a dark, criminal side was totally absurd. Besides which, the *evidence* made Brenda's theory ridiculous. Ned had blown the whistle on the scam—how could he have been involved in it?

"I mean, think about it," Brenda was saying. "It all fits so perfectly. Ned had to be in on it, don't you see? An insurance scam like this would need an insider."

Nancy stiffened as she caught Brenda's last words. "What was that?" she asked slowly.

"I said this job needed an insider," Brenda repeated. "I'm telling you, if you look in Ned's bank account, you'll find that missing fifty thousand. Hey, how's this for a headline—"

"Stop!" Nancy cried suddenly. She sprang up out of her chair. An inside job—of course!

In that instant everything fell neatly into place. She *knew* what had happened. She knew how and why Toby Foyle had been killed—*and* who had done it.

"Brenda, that's it!" Racing around to Brenda's side of the table, Nancy hugged the astonished reporter. "That's the answer. You got it!"

"I did?" For once in her life Brenda Carlton sounded uncertain.

"Yes. Ned is not a murderer," Nancy added quickly. "Look, I can't explain now. Do me a favor and go away, okay? I need to hurry if I'm going to get proof before Ned's hearing tomorrow."

Brenda's eyes narrowed. "Nancy Drew, are you throwing me out?" she demanded.

Nancy rolled her eyes. She didn't have time to argue! "I'm not throwing you out," she explained. "It's just that I have things to do."

"What about my story?" Brenda pressed her. "When do I get it?"

Nancy looked at her watch. It was three now. She bit her lip. "Give me until six o'clock tonight," she begged. "Then I'll give you the exclusive of your life, Brenda. This time I really mean it."

"Six o'clock? That won't give me much time to write the story," Brenda complained.

"I know you can do it," Nancy said firmly. She took Brenda's arm and practically pulled the young reporter to the door. "See you then."

Brenda was still protesting when Nancy closed the door on her, but at least she was gone. Nancy let out a sigh of relief, and leaned against the door, biting her thumbnail as she thought about how to proceed.

It had to be an inside job—with not two, but *three* people working together. Now it made sense!

At length she strode back into the kitchen. Lifting the receiver of the phone, she dialed the number for the Mutual Life Insurance Company.

"May I speak to Libby Cartwright?" Nancy asked when the receptionist answered.

"One moment," the receptionist said. There was a click and then Libby's high, girlish voice answered, "Accounting. Libby Cartwright speaking."

"Libby, it's Nancy Drew," Nancy said briskly. "I need to ask you one last question. Remember that story you told me about the man who lost his life savings when Mutual Life wouldn't pay his wife's hospital bills? Libby, who was that man?"

Five minutes later Nancy hung up the phone. There was a grim smile on her lips. Her conversation with Libby had confirmed one of her suspicions. Now she had to check out the other.

Straightening her shoulders, she picked up the receiver again. This time she dialed the Nickersons' number. Ned answered.

"It's me," Nancy said tersely. "I have a question for you. After I dropped you off last night, what did you do?"

"Do?" Ned sounded bewildered. "I went inside and watched TV, I think. Oh, and I called Mr. Packard. I told him we were back to investigating the insurance scam angle of Foyle's murder. I thought he ought to know."

Bingo! Nancy thought. "Did you happen to mention to him that I was going to see Mrs. Godfrey after I dropped you off?" she asked.

"Yeah, I think I did. Why?"

"Someone tried to run me down outside Mrs.

Godfrey's house last night," Nancy informed him.

"What? Are you all right? Nancy, what is this about?" Ned demanded. "What are you saying?"

Nancy exhaled slowly. "Brace yourself, Ned," she warned. "I believe Toby Foyle was killed by Joe Packard."

Chapter Sixteen

THERE WAS a long silence. Then Ned said, "If this is a joke, I don't think it's funny."

"I'm sorry, Ned," Nancy replied, and she meant it. "It isn't a joke."

"But *why?*" Ned's voice was raw with shock. "What possible reason could Joe Packard have for killing Toby Foyle?"

"It's a long story," Nancy told him, "and I'm still figuring out some of the details. How about if I come over and tell you in person?"

"I'll be waiting for you," Ned answered. He hung up with a click.

Nancy put down the receiver with a sigh and swept a hand through her hair. She wasn't looking forward to telling Ned this story. Packard was a respected figure at Mutual Life and practically a mentor to Ned. The truth was going to hurt.

When Nancy pulled up in front of Ned's house, he was sitting on the rail of his front porch, watching for her car.

"Let's talk out here," he said as she climbed the few steps to the porch. "My mom's home, and I don't want her to hear this conversation. At least, not until I'm sure you're right."

Nancy nodded and took a seat on the swing.

"Brenda Carlton, of all people, gave me the link I needed," she said matter-of-factly. "She was being her usual overdramatic self, talking about how the murder was part of a big criminal conspiracy. And she said the insurance fraud had to have been an inside job. That's when it hit me."

"What hit you?" asked Ned. "If all you're after is someone who works at the insurance company, why pick on Packard? There are a million other people I could more easily see as criminals. Wally Biggs, for example. Or Libby Cartwright. She was dating Foyle, after all."

Nancy ran a finger along the armrest of the swing. "But nobody else fits the way Packard does, Ned," she said softly. "Think about it. Who knew about your investigation of Foyle from the moment you started it? To whom did we tell all our suspicions about Michelle Ferraro and Dr. Meyers? Who tried to steer my investigation away from Meyers and toward Michelle?"

"Mr. Packard wasn't trying to steer us anywhere," Ned objected. "He was just giving his opinion. He never tried to convince you that he was right, did he?"

Nancy shook her head. "He was too smart to argue," she replied. "He knew that would only make me wonder why he cared so much. But I think he tried to convince me in other ways."

"What ways?" Ned jumped up and began pacing.

"On Monday morning I went to see Mr. Packard and told him two things," Nancy said. "First, I said that I'd just seen Michelle. He already knew about her coming at me with a knife. Second, I said that I was looking into the possibility of a Mutual Life employee being involved in the insurance scam with Foyle. Shortly after that, my car seat was slashed. I'm positive it was a move calculated to make me think of Michelle Ferraro, who'd recently attacked me with a knife." She smiled slightly. "It worked, too."

Ned's face was full of horror. "And the way your car was booby-trapped on Monday night," he murmured. "It was made to look as if someone who didn't know anything about cars had done it."

"Right," Nancy agreed. "And Mr. Packard lives right near you. Add to that the fact that he's the only one besides you and me who knew I'd be at Mrs. Godfrey's last night. It looks pretty bad for him, doesn't it?"

Suddenly Ned gave a fierce shake of his head. "Wait a minute. We're getting way ahead of ourselves," he said. "You still haven't explained the most important thing—his motive. Nancy, I can't believe Joe Packard would be involved in any scheme to defraud Mutual Life. He's spent his whole career *protecting* them from fraud!"

"That's the sad part," Nancy said. She took Ned's hand and pulled him down to sit beside her.

"Remember when you told me that Mr. Packard had changed since the death of his wife?" she asked. "You said it seemed as if he'd lost interest in his work. And everyone in the department was surprised that he took it so hard, since they'd been separated for some time."

Ned nodded. "I remember," he said, still obviously confused.

"Well, I don't think it was the loss of his wife that changed Mr. Packard," Nancy announced. She rocked the swing with her feet as she spoke. "I think it was what Mutual Life did to him then. In his eyes, the company betrayed him."

Ned scowled. "What are you talking about?"

"When I talked to Libby Cartwright, she told me a story she'd heard," Nancy said. "It was about a guy who had worked for the company all his life and whose wife had died after a long illness. Mutual Life refused to pay her medical expenses, and the man was stuck with them. His life savings were wiped out. I called Libby today and asked her who the man was."

She gazed at Ned and saw the growing realization in his brown eyes. "That's right. It was Joe Packard," she told him quietly.

Ned dropped his gaze and sat silently for a long moment. Thunder rumbled in the distance, and a warm, rain-scented breeze swept over the porch, ruffling his hair. At last he spoke. "So Packard decided to get revenge."

"I think so," said Nancy. "He's put his scheme together with Dr. Meyers, who'd been his wife's physician. Meyers was the middleman. He persuaded some of his patients to file false claims, and then he signed them. The claimants never asked for enough money to make the claims investigators at Mutual Life really suspicious."

"And with Packard heading up the claims investigation department," Ned put in, "it was simple to get the claims through." His eyes were flashing with anger now.

"Right," said Nancy, nodding. "Packard would just advise whoever the investigator was to settle, since fighting the claim legally would be time-consuming and probably more costly in the long run. No one would think of arguing with the boss—especially since he had a reputation as a company watchdog. If Joe Packard said it was all right, then it was all right."

Ned smiled bitterly. "Then I came along, with my gung-ho attitude, and nearly blew the whole scam," he said. "Packard must have flipped when he heard about my fight with Toby Foyle."

"I'm sure he did." Nancy tapped her fingers thoughtfully on her cheek. "I also suspect that Foyle was putting pressure on Meyers and, through Meyers, on Packard, to protect himself. He was really scared when you recognized him in that restaurant, Ned."

"Wow," Ned murmured, sounding dazed.

"Who could have guessed what it would lead to?" He stood up and began pacing again. "So now we need to figure out *how* Packard killed Foyle. And we have to prove it."

Nancy smiled. She was glad to see that Ned's mind was back on solving the case.

"As for how he did it," she said, leaning forward excitedly, "I think he called Foyle on Friday night, pretending he was Dr. Meyers, and set up a meeting for Saturday morning. He probably told Foyle that they shouldn't be seen together, since they were suspected of being in cahoots on the insurance scam. That's how he got Foyle to go out to the warehouse."

"How do you know all this?" Ned asked.

"Mrs. Godfrey told me a man named Meyers had called Foyle on her line Friday night. Now, Foyle had just recently gotten his own phone. It wasn't listed yet, but I know Dr. Meyers had the new number. So when I heard about this call, I thought, why would Meyers call on Mrs. Godfrey's line, and why would he tell her his name? It seemed kind of careless, for a man planning a murder." Nancy shrugged. "But it all makes sense—if you realize that someone was setting Dr. Meyers up as a scapegoat."

"Pretty smart, Drew," Ned commented, smiling down at her.

Nancy grinned back. "Thanks."

"You know the rest," she went on. "Packard went out early, parked in back of the warehouse, and waited for Foyle. When Foyle showed up,

Packard killed him, then left through the back door."

"And I just happened to show up a few seconds later," Ned added. "A nice bonus for Packard—I made a better scapegoat than Dr. Meyers." He shook his head angrily. "Okay, I'm convinced. But how do we prove it?"

"That's the hard part," Nancy admitted. She gazed at the lawn, where a few fat raindrops were beginning to fall. "But I have an idea. I think Packard made one mistake."

"Go on." Ned grabbed her hand.

"He has a habit of shredding cardboard matches when he's nervous," Nancy said. "When I was at the warehouse the other night I saw a bunch of little cardboard scraps on the floor. At the time I didn't think about them because the warehouse is full of cardboard boxes and a lot of them are falling apart. I'm sure that's what the police thought, too. But, see"—she raised one finger—"the boxes are brown cardboard, and some of the scraps I saw were gray. Like matches."

Ned's eyes lit up. "There's our proof!" he cried, pulling her to her feet. "Let's go get it!"

At that moment the front door opened and Mrs. Nickerson came out on the porch. "Ned, there's a phone call for you," she began.

"Not now, Mom," Ned said. He was already halfway down the porch steps. "Nancy and I have to get to the warehouse. She's solved the case!"

Mrs. Nickerson's mouth fell open. "Oh, how wonderful!" she exclaimed.

"I'll explain it all when we get back," Ned called as he and Nancy climbed into her Mustang.

"I just hope those scraps are still there," Nancy fretted as they drove toward the warehouse. "Someone might have cleaned them up."

"Don't even think about it," Ned said firmly. "We'll find them."

A few minutes later Nancy steered onto the gravelly parking area in front of the warehouse. She parked the car, and she and Ned jumped out. The sawhorses and police seals were still in place, she was glad to see. That meant no one had been allowed inside the warehouse since the crime.

After leading Ned to the ventilation duct, Nancy showed him how to crawl through. She followed and once again found herself in the dim interior of the big building.

There was a little daylight coming through the small windows set high up off the floor. Nancy and Ned quickly made their way back to the spot where Foyle's body had lain. Nancy shivered as she saw the chalked outline on the floor. It seemed even eerier now that she knew who had committed the crime.

Suddenly she heard a soft, shuffling noise coming from near the front of the building. She grabbed Ned's arm. "Did you hear that?" she whispered.

Ned nodded. For a long moment they stood motionless. Nancy strained her ears but didn't hear anything else. After a moment Ned shook his head. "Probably a rat," he told her.

"Yuck!" Nancy said, grimacing.

"It won't bother us," Ned assured her. "Now, where are those famous scraps of cardboard?"

Nancy knelt. "They were right by this box of receipts," she said, pointing to the battered box that lay on the floor near the chalked outline.

Ned squatted beside her and picked up a handful of little shreds. After a moment he gave a cry of triumph. "There's a gray one!" he announced. "When you look closely, you can see it was part of a match. Nancy, you were right! This proves Packard did it."

"How careless of me," a new voice suddenly cut in.

Nancy felt a sharp jolt of terror slice through her. Slowly she looked up.

Two men stood about ten feet away, gazing down at her and Ned. One of them was Dr. Meyers.

The other was Joe Packard. In his left hand was a big red gasoline can. And in his left hand was a small, deadly-looking gun—which was pointed at Nancy's heart.

Chapter Seventeen

NANCY FROZE. Beside her, she felt Ned tense, ready to spring forward. Packard immediately swung the gun and pointed it at him.

"I wouldn't try anything," he warned in a chilling voice. "I'm no marksman, but I doubt I could miss at this distance."

"Don't do it, Ned," Nancy said urgently.

"Very sensible," Packard told her. "Now get up, very slowly, and keep your hands where I can see them."

Ned and Nancy did as he instructed.

"If you don't mind my asking," said Nancy, forcing calm into her voice, "how did you know we were here?"

"Sheer luck," Packard replied. He set the gas can down at his side, never taking his eyes off the wo teenagers. "Ned's mother told me. 'They just eft for the warehouse. They say they've solved he crime,'" he added, mimicking Mrs. Nickerson's voice.

Ned gasped. "That was you on the phone, right before we left?"

Packard nodded. "I called to check up on you. It's a good thing I did, too. Otherwise we wouldn't have caught you in time," he said seriously. "I phoned Meyers and had him meet me here. We had to stop you kids before you got to the police."

Meyers cleared his throat and shifted his feet nervously. "Joe," he said, "let's cut the chatter and get this over with, okay?"

Nancy's heart plummeted. She'd been dreading those words. "Uh—how exactly do you plan to stop us?" she asked, trying to keep her voice even. Her eyes shifted to the five-gallon can of gasoline. Was he going to kill them and then set fire to the building? She glanced around, looking for some way to escape, but there was none—as long as Packard kept that gun trained on them.

Packard gazed at her sadly. "It's not a pleasant topic," he murmured. "I'm sure you'd rather not know."

That made Nancy mad. "I know you're planning to kill us," she retorted. "Why are you being so delicate? Are you afraid you might hurt our feelings?"

"Please." Packard frowned. "Believe me, I didn't want this." He looked at Ned. "I did everything I could to stop you from getting into

trouble. But you just kept prying into things tha
didn't concern you."

"If you're talking about my investigation o
Toby Foyle, I was just doing my job," Ned sai
angrily. "The way *you* taught me to do it, Mr
Packard. You fraud!" he suddenly burst out. "
can't believe I ever looked up to you. All this tim
I thought you were such a good man, and now i
turns out you're just a murdering crook!"

Packard's neck swelled with anger. "I am not
crook!" he raged. "I was just taking back wha
was mine. I devoted my life to that company, an
they showed their appreciation by robbing me.
ask you, was that justice?"

Nancy couldn't believe the warped thing
Packard was saying. "Was it justice when yo
took Toby Foyle's life?" she demanded.

Packard's gaze shifted to her. Keeping her eye
locked on his, she continued, "And was it justic
when you tried to frame your friend Dr. Meyers
I doubt he'd agree with you."

"Be quiet!" Packard thundered, but it was to
late. Meyers was staring at him in horror.

"Joe!" Meyers cried. "Is that true?"

"Oh, didn't Mr. Packard tell you?" Nancy
asked. She put a sarcastic note into her voice.
"He called Foyle's landlady and pretended he
was you, so that if the murder was ever linked to
your scam, you'd be the one to take the fall."

"That's enough!" barked Packard. He backed
up in a sudden movement and waved the gun at
Meyers. "Get over there with the kids, Bob. I
hoped to spare you, but now I see it's not

practical." He raised the red can and began to sprinkle the rows of cardboard boxes. The strong smell of gasoline filled the air.

"No—Joe, please!" Meyers begged.

Suddenly Nancy heard the soft, shuffling sound again. This time it was much nearer. Packard must have heard it, too, she realized. He paused, cocking his head.

"What was that?" he asked sharply.

"Just a rat," Ned replied, his voice filled with contempt. "You're in good company."

"Eeeek!"

Nancy jumped as a shrill scream suddenly tore the air. A noise of tumbling boxes came from behind Packard. He whipped around, a startled look on his face.

Nancy took her chance. Like a shot, she raced forward, covering in two strides the distance to where Packard stood. Even as he swung the gun around to cover her again, her foot lashed up and out in a swift kick. The gun flew out of Packard's hand, and he gave a shout of rage.

Ned was right beside Nancy. "Let me," he told her, drawing back his arm. Before Packard could react, Ned's fist smashed into his jaw.

The blow must have had all the power of Ned's anger behind it, for Packard swayed and toppled to the floor, out cold. Ned rubbed his fist, looking pleased and surprised.

Suddenly out of the corner of her eye Nancy spotted Dr. Meyers reaching for Packard's gun. He was too far away for her to stop him. "Ned, get Meyers!" she shouted.

Ned made a flying leap. Just as the doctor's fingers were about to close on the gun, Ned knocked him to the floor. He drew back his fist again.

"Don't hit me. I give up!" Meyers cried, covering his face with his hands.

As soon as she was sure that Ned had Meyers under control, Nancy stepped cautiously toward the place from where the scream had come. Who—or what—had made all that racket?

Suddenly a dark form crept out from behind a stack of boxes, and Nancy's breath caught in her throat.

"Nancy, is that you?" came Brenda Carlton's terrified voice.

Nancy's jaw dropped. "Brenda!" she exclaimed. "What on earth are you doing here?"

Brenda kept moving forward, and Nancy could see that her dark eyes were round with fear. "Wh-where's the rat?" the reporter stammered.

Suddenly Nancy understood what the sounds and screaming had been. She began to laugh.

"So that was *you,*" she said. "Brenda, we heard you moving around. Ned told Packard the noise was a rat, and you heard the word *rat* and screamed. There *is* no rat, silly! Now, please tell me what you're doing here."

Brenda looked embarrassed for a second, but then she gave a smug smile. "I followed you from River Heights," she replied. "I wanted to make sure I got my story. I had just sneaked into this place, to see what you and Ned were doing, when those two men arrived. So I followed them to find out what they were up to. I was trying to get just a little closer when you guys heard me. I was worried about the range of this thing." She held up a portable tape recorder. "But I think I got it all."

For the second time that day Nancy hugged Brenda Carlton. "Brenda, I love you!" she cried. "You distracted the crooks, and you got their confessions on tape. Now, if you'll just do me a favor and go get the police, I'll honestly be able to say that you saved the day!"

"Oh, Ned, it's so great that you're cleared," Bess said. "I only wish I'd been allowed in for the grand jury hearing this morning."

It was early Thursday afternoon, and Nancy, Bess, Ned, and George were at Mama's restaurant for the promised victory pizza.

On her way to Mama's, Nancy had stopped at a newsstand and bought a copy of *Today's Times,* the paper that Brenda Carlton wrote for. Once they were seated, she pulled out the newspaper and unfolded it. She wanted to see what Brenda had written about the Foyle case.

"Read it aloud, Nancy," George urged her. "This should be good for a laugh."

"Listen to this headline: 'Foyle Killer Foiled at Last!' " Nancy quoted. Everyone at the table groaned. Nancy grinned and read on: " 'In a dramatic scene witnessed by this reporter, the mysterious case of the murder of Toby Foyle came to a close yesterday. Mapleton Police arrested Joseph Packard, head of the claims investigation department at the Mutual Life Insurance Company. Packard is charged with the murder of Foyle and also with insurance fraud, vandalism, arson, and several counts of attempted murder. Also charged in the insurance fraud is Dr. Robert S. Meyers.

" 'Hometown hero Ned Nickerson (see photo) is breathing easier today, thanks to the efforts of this reporter. Nickerson, who also works in the claims investigation department at Mutual Life, had been the prime suspect in the slaying of Foyle. He and Foyle were known to have quarreled, and Nickerson was found at the scene of the crime. However, clues led this reporter to suspect that the real explanation for the homicide lay elsewhere.' "

"Oh, this is too much! 'Clues' didn't lead Brenda Carlton anywhere," Bess declared. "Nancy is the one who cracked the case."

"*Shhh.* Let Nancy finish reading the story," Ned told Bess. "Go on, Nan."

" 'The incredible truth: Foyle, Packard, and Meyers were part of an alleged criminal conspiracy to defraud the Mapleton insurance company. Nickerson was an innocent pawn, caught in their deadly game. Again, clues led this reporter to a warehouse on the outskirts of Mapleton, where Packard and his associate had allegedly lured Nickerson and his girlfriend, Nancy Drew (see photo), apparently intending to kill them. Fortunately for the two teens, this reporter was able to distract the alleged killers until Nickerson could overpower them. Shortly afterward the police arrived on the scene, alerted by this reporter.' "

Nancy folded the paper and laid it aside. "That's basically it," she said. "The rest is just about how Mutual Life is investigating the insurance fraud and how there are a couple of other people involved."

" 'Clues led this reporter,' " George muttered. "I don't believe it! Just substitute 'Nancy Drew' for 'clues' wherever it appears, and you might begin to understand what really happened."

Nancy laughed. "This is one story I don't begrudge Brenda," she said. "If it hadn't been for her, Ned and I might not be sitting here right now. Of course, everything she did was completely accidental, but still, I have to say I'm feeling pretty friendly toward Brenda right now."

At that moment their waitress set a huge, steaming pizza on the table in front of them. "Here you are—one pie with the works," she announced. "Say, aren't you the guy who they thought killed that other guy in a warehouse?" she asked, staring at Ned.

Ned looked warily at her, and Nancy could see him tensing up. "Why do you ask?"

"I read all about the case in the paper this morning—how you nearly went to jail for someone else's crime and how that reporter saved you. Congratulations," the waitress told him. "You're a lucky guy."

After she had gone, Ned reached out and grasped Nancy's hand. "I *am* a lucky guy," he said softly. "I don't think the waitress knows quite how lucky I am."

"George, don't look. I think they're about to get mushy," Bess remarked.

Nancy smiled into Ned's eyes. "Ned, what are you talking about?" she asked, batting her lashes coyly.

Ned laughed. Then he leaned over and kissed Nancy on the lips. "I think you know what I mean. I'm the luckiest guy in the world—because I've got Nancy Drew for a girlfriend!"

Nancy's next case:

The headline-grabbing letter in Brenda Carlton's advice column has stirred up a hornet's nest in River Heights, and someone's bound to get stung. The unsigned letter is from a woman who claims she's about to be murdered—by her own husband! Nancy must find the woman *and* find out if she's really in danger.

The evidence indicates that Mrs. Keating, the wife of a prominent banker, wrote the letter. After a car accident with Brenda, Mrs. Keating claims that her brake lines were cut. Now it's up to Nancy to uncover the proof. A false accusation could ruin Mr. Keating's career . . . or cost Mrs. Keating her life . . . in *POISON PEN,* Case #60 in The Nancy Drew Files™.